WESTERHAM WITCHES AND A VENETIAN VENDETTA

Paranormal Investigation Bureau Book 15

DIONNE LISTER

Dionne Lister

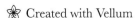 Created with Vellum

This book is dedicated to all those tireless emergency service workers who, at times, sacrifice their sanity and safety to help their communities. To the police, paramedics, doctors and nurses, and firemen and women who risk themselves every day to keep strangers safe, thank you. You are appreciated.

CHAPTER 1

I shut my eyes and angled my face up towards the sun. The comforting warmth and kiss of a gentle breeze on my skin sure felt like freedom. I grinned.

Regula Pythonissam was dead, finished, kaput.

I had my old life back. Well… not exactly my *old*, old life. It was something even better because it had magic and my mother and the ability to go wherever I wanted without worrying I'd be struck dead at any moment. Oh, and squirrels, lots and lots of squirrels. Speaking of which, there was a gentle tap, tap, tap on my hand. I opened my eyes.

Roger, the grey squirrel with one white paw, blinked up at me from his spot on the outdoor table. He'd left his seat at the mini-picnic table where thirteen of his friends sat, nibbling on nuts. I chuckled. They were so freaking adorable that I almost couldn't stand it. There were still nuts in Roger's bowl, though. "I'm not sure what you want, sweetie. You've still got food. You don't feel sick or anything, do you?" I had no idea if he could understand me. One of these days I'd figure out how to talk to animals, dammit. "Hang on a minute." I visualised me leaving and coming back. Even if I couldn't pick anything up, didn't mean the squirrels couldn't pick up on what I was thinking.

I gave Roger a soft pat on the head, and he closed his eyes. Hmm, he seemed to like it, so I kept stroking him. He chirped. Ooh, maybe that's what he wanted. Aw. "Way to melt my heart, little guy." Another squirrel, with a little triangle missing from the side of her ear, who I'd named Scrappy, jumped off the squirrel-sized bench seat and scurried to me. She craned her head up to look at me with large, dark eyes. "Do you want a pat too?" She chittered. I giggled. This was awesome times one hundred. I scratched her head with my other hand. She closed her eyes and made cute squirrely noises. It was as if I'd died and gone to my version of heaven. Thankfully, I'd survived Dana, her father, and their minions, and this was real life.

Good guys did win sometimes.

Footsteps sounded on the garden path behind me. I turned my head just enough to see who it was—I didn't want to stop patting my jittery friends in case they ran away because of the newcomer.

My mother, her auburn hair cut into a shoulder-length bob, approached, Will at her side. He had a bemused look on his face, but my mother's forehead wrinkled. She blinked; then a smile quirked up one side of her mouth. "Ah, what's going on here, then?" After being held captive for so long in the UK by Dana's father, a slight English accent had crept into her voice, refining the relaxed Aussie edges.

Will grinned. "Lily's hanging out with her comrades. She's building a squirrel army to help defend her."

"Hey, I am not. Well, not anymore. They're just my friends, and we're enjoying a farewell brunch together. Maybe one day I'll need them to take up arms for my cause, but now the RP thing is behind us, the army thing is on the back-burner." I grinned. Both squirrels chittered, and they sounded annoyed. Oops, I'd stopped patting them. Yikes. I got back to it. "Demanding little beasties, aren't you?"

Mum and Will sat on either side of me at the picnic table. Mum slowly reached out and patted Roger. "So, we have some good news."

Seemed like my life was full of good news lately, and I was not complaining. Not. At. All. "And what's that?"

"I'm coming on holiday with you all." Her wide smile filled my heart with joy.

Wow, that was some news. Ever since we'd saved her a few weeks ago, she'd been wary and staying close to home. This was the best surprise ever. I threw my arms around her. "Woohoo! That's awesome news!" My loud, flamboyant celebrations startled the squirrels. They all took off, scampering and leaping in every direction until there weren't any left on the table. A couple of little squirrel bowls had turned over in the chaos, seeds scattering everywhere. Oops.

Will chuckled. "Yeah, they'd make a great army. So steadfast and brave."

My mother snorted. So, that's who I got it from. I shrugged, pretending everything was fine. "So, they need some training. I still believe in them and my vision for a furry ninja cohort of armed squirrels."

Mum patted my hand. "That's my girl, stubborn and persistent." Her eyes glistened, and she blinked back tears. "Thank you for never giving up on me and your father. I know he'd be so proud of you." She shook her head. "I never stopped believing you and James would find me." She squeezed my hand as I blinked away my own tears.

"None of us gave up. James, Beren, Will, Imani, Ma'am, Mill, Liv, everyone was in it for as long as it took. If it weren't for them, we wouldn't have gotten there." I sniffled before snot ran out of my nose. Real classy. "Anyway, let's not talk about that now. We have a holiday to go on!"

Mum grinned. "We sure do. I'm packed and ready. Everyone else left just before we came outside. Are you ready?"

Argh, I didn't get to say goodbye to my furry buddies properly. Oh, well. They'd come back once I returned, I supposed. I magicked their tiny bowls away but left the seeds littering the table. They could finish it off after we left. We all stood, and excitement bubbled in my stomach. It was time to have a holiday. Finally.

Venice, here we come.

CHAPTER 2

D ana's dad had burned my mother's magic out. She had access to the portal of magic, but she couldn't suck in more than a drip at a time—it was never enough to do anything, so she came through my doorway wheeling her suitcase into the Hotel Delfino reception room. We hurried out of the way so that Will could come through.

The room had a moderately sloping terrazzo floor adorned with a red Persian rug. Two red love seats sat against one wall, their ornate gilded arms and legs a bit gaudy for my taste. Blue-blown-glass sconces with golden fittings were affixed to the wall on either side of the door. I smiled at the ancient scent of old building and furnishings. We were really here, on holiday in Venice. Venice! "Eek! I can't wait to go exploring, and we have to go on a gondola, plus the glass-blowing. I've always wanted to see that."

Mum laughed. "You were always Miss Enthusiastic. Just hold your horses for five minutes." She pressed the brass door-bell. Its shrill ring made me jump, even though I'd known it was coming. I rolled my eyes at myself. "I see you're still as jumpy as ever."

"Yep. Some things never change." Not for the first time since we had my mother back did I wonder at it. Was she really here making references to the past? I reached out and touched her arm. She gave me a quizzical look. "Just checking you're really here." I smiled.

She returned my smile. "Yes, and I'm not going anywhere… well, except if you go on holidays and invite me."

"Sounds good to me."

The door opened. A short elderly lady, her white hair gathered into a single plait that hung over her shoulder and descended to her waist, smiled, her wrinkles wrinkling. Her light-blue eyes sparkled. "Buongiorno. Welcome to Hotel Delfino." Her strong voice had that crackly quality old people's voices tended to acquire. She must have been in her mid eighties at least. I hoped I was standing that straight if… when I got to her age. At least with RP and Piranha gone, that chance had increased exponentially.

"Buongiorno, Signora." Mum smiled. "*Sono* Katerina Bianchi. This is my daughter, Lily, and her partner, William." My mother's Italian wasn't fluent, but I knew she'd learned some when she and my father had gotten engaged. I supposed she figured they would visit Italy every now and again.

"Please, come in. I'm Isabella." The old lady stepped back and held the door wide. She turned to look behind her, lifted her arm, and clicked her fingers a couple of times. "Francesco! *Sprigati!*" A skinny young man dressed in black trousers and a short-sleeve white shirt answered her summons. He bowed his head quickly. She said something else to him in Italian, and he nodded. Magic tickled my scalp, and all our suitcases disappeared. So, that's how they did things in a witch-only hotel.

Isabella turned back to us. She handed my mother one key and me another. "Your bags have been sent to your rooms—on the first floor to the right. Breakfast is served between seven and ten in the morning. If you have any questions, just call reception. Enjoy your stay."

Will grabbed my hand as we followed my mother along the hallway to a timber staircase that also seemed to be on an angle. I tilted my head to the side. "Is it my imagination or—"

Will chuckled. "Not your imagination. Venice is sinking. Things are bound to be a bit crooked."

"Why don't witches subtly fix it?" We collectively had so much power, surely something could be done to at least stop the iconic city's demise.

Mum started up the stairs. "I'm afraid it's such a huge undertaking, that it would be hard to hide that witches existed. Even if we managed to come up with a plan and orchestrate it, non-witches would ask a lot of questions. We couldn't stop it with an invisible barrier—there would need to be structures put into place under the buildings. Rather obvious and not an option."

Mum stopped at the first-floor landing. There were two hallways—one leading to the left and one to the right, but, as Isabella had explained, we needed to go right. We followed Mum along the narrow, red-carpeted hallway. Cream-and-gold-striped wallpaper gave it a '70s feel, and more of the Venetian glass scones lit our way. Even so, it was quite dark with no natural light, not that it felt creepy—the atmosphere was more of a cosy, "Wow, I'm in Italy" one. The buzz of adventure hummed in my body, and I couldn't wait to see our room, then the rest of Venice.

Mum stopped in front of a door and looked at me. "This is mine. Well, mine and Angelica's." She was sharing with

Angelica because she still felt vulnerable. Even with the counselling she was doing, it would take time for her to recover. In the meantime, we were all doing our bit to help. Since we'd saved her, she'd lived with us at Angelica's, in the room next to Will and me. She had nightmares almost every night. Her anguished cries for help and calling out for my father broke my heart. After the first couple of times, I'd gone in there to wake her and reassure her, she seemed to be more upset about waking me than having the nightmare. She'd explained that her nightmares had started when she'd been kidnapped and had never stopped. The enormity of that had left me angry at RP all over again and heartbroken at what she'd suffered and still did. Angelica had suggested a mind wipe, but my mother refused. My thought was to try and create a spell that could stop the bad dreams. I wasn't sure how, exactly, so I hadn't said anything, but I was working on it.

The door opened, and Angelica stood there smiling. "Ah, you made it. Lovely. Your bag's already here." She moved back and opened the door wider for my mother to enter.

Will had walked to the next door. "This is ours, Lily."

I smiled at him. "Cool." I looked back at Angelica. "What's the plan for today? Are we going to all go for a walk and ease into things?"

Angelica smiled. "Yes, dear. I think we should start with a visit to Piazza San Marco and get an ice cream. It's rather warm outside."

"Sounds like a plan." I gave Mum a small wave. "See you soon. Meet you downstairs in ten minutes?"

Angelica nodded. "Okay. I'll let the others know." We'd set up a Facebook chat for our group so we could keep tabs on where everyone was. That way, we'd be able to organise group things, but if someone didn't want to come, we'd still know what they were up to.

Will held the door open for me. As I scooted past him, he smacked my bottom. "Ow!"

The door closed. "What do you mean, ow? I hardly tapped you."

"Yeah, I know, but you scared me. I wasn't expecting it, and that was my reaction."

He shook his head, smiling. "Of course. Silly me for forgetting you have at least one surprise-induced heart attack every day."

"More evidence that I was a squirrel in a former life. Genetic memory is a thing, you know." I held back a laugh, keeping my expression as serious as possible.

He nodded thoughtfully. "That makes total sense. Another mystery bites the dust." He took in the room. "Quaint and very Venetian."

"It is." I plonked onto the double bed and tried bouncing. "Not bad. I love the terrazzo floors, even if they are sloping just a smidge." I hopped up. "What's our view like?" I hurried to the window and looked out at a white-paved courtyard enclosed by three-storey walls on all sides. The space was a large square, maybe five by five metres. Tables and chairs sat under red-and-blue-striped umbrellas. A few people occupied those tables, having a meal and chatting while pigeons poked around their feet for scraps, some braver pigeons daring to alight on the tables of patrons still eating. So peaceful and holidayish. I grinned. This week away was going to be phenomenal.

A man with thick, dark hair and dressed in similar black slacks and white shirt as our bellboy this morning strode out of the door, a scowl on his face. He waved his arms in the air. His voice was loud but not quite shouting. "Shoo! *Va via! Va Via! Uccelli disgustosi.*" He approached one of the tables and kicked his foot under it. Oh, that's what he was doing. The pigeons flew away from him but settled across the courtyard. He made a strangled sound and slammed his hands on his hips and glared at the pigeons. Magic tingled my scalp.

The birds flapped crazily, taking off and flying away. Feathers floated around the courtyard as if there'd just been a massive pillow fight. The diners waved their arms around their faces to clear the air. When everything settled, three little bodies lay on the ground. I frowned. *How sad. What a meanie.* "This isn't the best start to our holiday."

Will had been peering over my shoulder. "They carry lice and leave a mess. Trust me; you don't want them around where you're eating."

"Yes, but did he have to kill them?"

"He didn't kill all of them."

I deepened my frown and directed it at Will.

He shrugged one shoulder. "What? It could've been worse." He shook his head. "Look at it this way; our holiday can only get better from here, right?"

I rolled my eyes. "Now you've probably jinxed us. What if it doesn't get better?"

He raised a brow, grabbed me around the waist, and pulled me to him for a kiss. "Hey, we're together in one of the most beautiful cities in the world. Let's focus on that." I was about to answer, but he placed his lips over mine and kissed the words away.

When the kiss was over, I sighed at the smile I couldn't help—I wanted to be annoyed at his lack of sympathy for the pigeons, but his kiss had disarmed me. "Okay. You win. Let's go meet the others and have that ice cream." I took off the jacket I'd worn from the UK—because, let's face it, it was still cold over there—and grabbed my phone rather than the Nikon before going downstairs. Today was supposed to be a pleasant twenty-six Celsius and sunny in Venice—perfect weather for being out and about, and whilst I loved taking photos, the middle of the day wasn't the best lighting, so the phone would do for some quick snaps.

Under the foyer's ornate Venetian chandelier that depicted flowers holding the globes, a group chatted. I grinned and hurried over, throwing my arms around the nearest person. "Liv! Eek!"

She hugged me back. "Lily! Yay! This is going to be awesome."

"I know, right?"

Will shook Beren's hand, and they slapped each other's backs in a thumpingly loud man hug. Why couldn't they just do gentle? Why did there have to be a show of "look how strong and robust we are. We can slap hard and take a slapping in return." I chuckled. Ah, men.

"Surprise!" A duo of voices came from behind me.

I spun around, and my eyes widened. My mouth dropped open. "Sarah! Lavender!" They threw their arms around me in a group hug. "What are you guys doing here?" When I'd initially spoken to Will's sister about coming on holiday, she'd told me she and Lavender had work already booked, but they'd try and join us for lunch or dinner one day.

Sarah grinned. "The job we had got postponed. We needed sun, and it's pouring today. It's forecast to rain all week, actually. We might get called away if it fines up, but for now, we're holidaying."

"It's so good to see you both." I hadn't seen them since the day they helped us smash RP apart. They'd both risked their lives for the cause, and they weren't even agents. "How is everything?"

They shared an excited look. Hmm. They gave each other a nod, and Lavender turned to me. "We're agents in training."

"W—what?!" Oh, no. Didn't I have enough loved ones to worry about?

Sarah grinned. "We're going to be part-time and still do our fashion stuff on the side. We'll be overflow agents when there are special cases. I think they want us for undercover stuff since we don't look like agents at all. And after losing so many agents in the RP war, they need new recruits." Not only had RP murdered agents when we attacked, some of the agents at headquarters and in Paris and Germany had been arrested afterwards for being secret RP members. They were pretty sure they'd uncovered all of them, but, unfortunately, we couldn't be certain. And now, of course, they were super short-staffed.

"I can't believe Chad is caving and putting more people on." Unbelievably, he still had his job, and although Angelica had *a* job back, she'd been relegated to a position under my brother. It was utterly ridiculous. I'd asked her about it, but she'd told me not to worry and that someone was working on things behind the scenes. For the PIB's sake, I sure hoped so. With the lack of funding and massive agent shortage, how long could they effectively fight crime?

Lavender made a tut-tut noise. "Don't be silly, darling. We're going to be working for the Paris office."

"Right, well, Agent Roche is a good egg, so that makes sense. But please, please, please stay safe. Do you know how many people I've got to worry about?" Yes, I was making this about me, but after the year I'd had, surely some consideration was owed to my frayed nerves.

Lavender linked his arm through mine. "We'll be most careful, Lilykins. And if we feel like we're in over our heads, we know who to call." He gave me a wink.

I groaned. "I've had enough battles to last a lifetime. I'm pretty sure killing Dana was me hitting my peak." I still wasn't sure how I'd managed to kill her when she had her return to sender up. Angelica had theorised that in her grief and fear, she wasn't focussing her magic properly. There was also the fact that I was, apparently, one of the most powerful witches of our time, and in a battle of return to senders, the most powerful witch won. Turns out, that was me. Suck it, Piranha! To deflect any unwanted attention I might have received over being so powerful, we'd explained killing Dana as having been a joint-witch effort since no one from outside our trusted group actually saw what happened.

Lavender pouted. "But you wouldn't just leave us to die, would you?"

I frowned. "Of course not."

He patted my hand. "Good. That's all I needed to know." Sarah grinned.

"Argh! I'm such a sucker, aren't I?"

She shrugged. "Maybe… but it's why we love you. You just can't help helping."

"Hey, people." Imani appeared out of the hubbub of everyone catching up. We returned her greeting, and there were more hugs. Talk about a hugfest. As much as I loved my friends, maybe we could call a moratorium on hugs for the remainder of the holiday. I'd had my monthly quota of them this morning.

Angelica clapped loudly, getting everyone's attention. "Time to get this show on the road, people." It was weird to see her in holiday-type clothes. If she wasn't wearing her PIB uniform, she was always in something staid, like dark trousers and a grey, white or black collared shirt. Today, she wore flowy navy-blue pants and a navy-blue-and-white-striped sleeveless shirt with a low scooped neckline. Very summery. Her hair was still in its well-behaved bun though, which was probably a good thing, or we wouldn't recognise her. I laughed to myself as we filed out the front double doors and into a large stone-paved square. Mmm, the warmth was good. Although the smell was… a bit off. Not terribly, but it wasn't exactly fresh air. I'd heard about that. The canals usually smelled when it was warm. Oh well, a small price to pay for the Venetian experience.

Clusters of holidaymakers in bright, happy summer clothes strolled through the square, others—maybe people who lived here—stood in small groups, talking. This square seemed to be all hotels and homes—units, probably. Some buildings were brick and some were rendered but rundown looking, bits of render missing to reveal the red brick beneath.

Angelica led us across the paved expanse to a bridge. On the other side of the bridge, the pathway narrowed to only a few feet across and slid between buildings. The sun disappeared as shadows swallowed us. We had to walk two abreast to allow for the people coming the other way. And there were no cars. I knew there wouldn't be cars, but seeing it was another thing. So weird, but so cool. Shopfronts crowded both sides of the path. Gift shops, mostly, and glass vendors selling Murano wares. I didn't want to buy anything here though—I wanted to visit the island and see the glass-blowing for myself and maybe buy something directly from there, although it wouldn't hurt to check out prices here before we went. You never knew.

Lavender still had his arm linked in mine. Liv spoke from behind us. "Isn't this exciting! I can't believe we're here."

I smiled, and the warm buzz of happiness filled my insides. We really were here, and so was Mum. She was walking at the front of our group, next to Angelica. It was still hard to believe she was alive. "I know. It's so old and so very different to the UK." *And I never thought I'd get here.* As much as I'd believed we'd eventually beat Dana and her father, I also believed I'd die doing it… or at least one of us would. How were we all still alive?

We turned a corner into another shadowed alleyway, shops and restaurants on both sides. It was beginning to feel like an ancient, endless shopping district. Still, the old, and yes, still-crooked buildings, were totally charming. We rounded another corner, a steady stream of people coming the other way. Such a hub of activity.

A tall archway, part of a dirty, rendered building, stood in front of us, a blue clock with golden stars set into it above a first-floor window. Dirty sounded as if I was being rude, but they probably left it like that on purpose. It gave the place atmosphere—some would call it patina. In Sydney, we'd call it neglect, but this wasn't Sydney, and I loved it. "Oh, is that a twenty-four-hour clock?" There were definitely twenty-four roman numerals around the blue disk instead of twelve.

Angelica looked up. "Yes, dear. There's a bigger one on the other side of the tower. It was built at the very end of the fifteenth century. Pretty, isn't it?"

"Very."

We walked under the arch and into the famed Saint Mark's Square. There was so much to take in. The great open expanse was hemmed in on most sides by grand buildings with archways framing covered walkways. Crowds had half-filled the square, pigeons taking up the rest of the available ground space, and that wasn't enough. Pigeons sat on some people's heads and shoulders. Holy moly. As cute as it was, Will's earlier comment about lice had me scratching the back of my neck. "Ew, is that sanitary?"

"What, lovie?" Lavender asked.

"The pigeons crawling all over people."

He chuckled. "That's just part of Venice's charm. I have to say, out of everything you could be looking at, that's got your attention?"

"Um… yes?" I was hopeless.

"Instead of worrying about those flying rats, why don't you check out Saint Mark's Basilica?" He nodded at a striking building to our left. Wow. The large stone building had massive archways, some inset with artwork of people in flowy robes. Lots of pointy bits graced the top of the building—yes, my descriptive powers would probably embarrass a five-year-old. The humungous domes added even more grandeur, and then there was the golden lion sculpture in the middle above what I guessed was the main entry. Oh, and let's not forget the angels above that. Talk about building something to impress the masses. I couldn't wait to come back at sunset and take some photos. The diffused golden light would make for some incredible shots.

The sharp sound of flapping surrounded us as a flock of pigeons took off. Small grey and white feathers floated around us. I sucked in a quick breath, and my mouth fell open. I squeezed my eyes shut. "Lavender…."

"Yes, lovie."

"Please look at my head and tell me there's no bird poo on it." After a long moment of silence, I opened my eyes and looked at him. "Well, is there?" If there was, I did not want to feel for it and get crap all over my hand.

I needn't have asked though. A young couple standing near us were staring at me and laughing. *Yeah, very funny.* I looked at them with my other sight. Non-witches. So I couldn't even magic it away. Damn it!

"Sorry, honey. They got you."

"Damn birds." I sighed. "I'm going to go back to the hotel to magic it off. Will you wait for me?"

"Of course. But you know that it's good luck."

I raised my brow and folded my arms in front of my chest. "I can't believe you said that. Yes, that's the consolation prize because who wouldn't be happy at getting shat on. Seriously, Lav? It's not like I just won a million dollars. I have bird crap *in my hair.* I'm pretty sure you and everyone else here who didn't get pooed on are the lucky ones."

Will, who'd stopped behind us while chatting to Beren, came to stand in front of me. "What's wro—" His gaze made it to the top of my head. "Oh." He was normally a master at the poker face, but his ability must have been on holiday as well. He scrunched his face in an "ew" way. "You have some on your shoulder too."

"Of course I do." The people who'd been laughing had shuffled over a few steps so they could still see me past Will. They were still snickering. Poo heads. Oh, no, that would be me. Damn. If only I could talk to animals, I'd be requesting a special pigeon delivery on their heads too. Where was Millicent when I needed her? Unfortunately, she and James couldn't make it. One of Millicent's best friends was getting married this coming weekend, and she was the maid of honour, plus, the PIB had been so short-staffed. James had wanted to stay at work and make sure the case against the remaining RP members was built with precision. And, not that I knew for sure, but I would bet that Angelica had wanted him there to be her eyes and ears as well. Anyway, no Millicent meant no revenge bird poo, so I glared at them instead because smiting was frowned upon.

Will stared at me, then turned his head to see what I was glaring at. He looked back at me. "Why don't we go and get you cleaned up." He held out his hand for me. I took it.

"Okay." I turned to Lavender. "Don't go too far. We'll be back in a few minutes." At least we could magic me clean as soon as we walked in the hotel door. Staying at a witchy hotel was such a great idea. At least Liv and everyone else were too busy being impressed by the scenery to notice my predicament.

Will and I hurried back the way we'd come. I was glad he was with me because I'd probably get lost. The narrow passageways all looked the same. I'd have to remember the different shops. I was betting that Google maps didn't work well in this rabbit warren. Other than everything being so close together, the tightly packed buildings probably disrupted the internet.

When we reached the hotel, Will opened the door for me. "Dirty ladies first."

I stopped in front of Will and gave him a look that promised violence. He smirked. Right. I lowered my chin to my chest and shoved my head onto his chest and rubbed. When I was done, I smiled innocently up at him. "Anything else you'd like to say?"

He frowned at the white bird poo smeared on his black T-shirt. "No. I think that's about it."

"Thought so." I snorted. There was nothing like sharing

the grossness with the one you loved, especially when they deserved it.

Rather than magic the dirt off near the front door where non-witches might see us, we walked down the hallway. Two different magics pinged me. Staying in a witch-friendly place was going to take some getting used to. Even though my friends and family used magic around me, it was familiar. New magic was always more jarring in its vibrations. It was like the difference between having soothing background music on compared to something with an ear-splitting, body-vibrating bass.

At the end of the hallway, we stopped near a fake plant that sat in one corner next to a white door with a gold-coloured sign that had *Ufficio* in bold black lettering. Well, that wasn't hard to understand. It looked so similar to *office* that you couldn't go wrong.

I was about to magic the poo off my head when raised voices came from the ufficio—a woman's voice, followed quickly by a man's. Will and I looked at each other. They were arguing in Italian, so we couldn't understand what they said. At least, I assumed they were arguing. Italians were enthusiastic verbal communicators, but surely that level of yelling wasn't normal.

Will and I looked at each other. I lowered my voice. "We can't really do this here, then. They'll feel our magic and think we're eavesdropping. It would be totally awkward."

"Agreed." Will looked around and gave a nod at another door halfway back to the main staircase. "Why don't we try that door there. It probably leads to the courtyard." I nodded, and we turned, the shouting still pulsing from the office. We hurried towards the other door, and just as Will opened it, a man burst out of the office and stomped down the hallway, staring at the ceiling and talking to himself, his hands gesturing "why?"

An attractive middle-aged woman stood in the doorway and glowered at him, her lips pinched together. She saw us and did a double take before schooling her expression. Her fake smile came through loud and clear before she stepped back into the office and shut the door.

Will gave me a "yikes" look and opened the door. "Gorgeous ladies first." He smiled.

"You're a fast learner." I grinned and stepped past him into another, shorter hallway that led to a door that was propped open, revealing the courtyard beyond. There was no need to go out there, though, now that the drama was over. I opened myself to my magic and willed the poo away, envisioning the courtyard pavers. I looked up at Will, whose shirt was clean. "Is it gone?" My magic was awesome, but I'd never tried to remove poo from my hair before. Better to be safe than touching it and being sorry.

He nodded. "Ready to resume our holiday?"

"You bet."

We'd had dead pigeons, and I'd been pooed on. Bad stuff supposedly came in threes, but I was going to stay positive. At least the bad things had been fairly minor, so there was nothing to worry about. Nothing at all.

CHAPTER 3

"Well, today was awesome." Clean and happy after my shower, I slid into the crisp, white sheets next to Will and yawned. The bedside clock read 23:19.

"We certainly made the most of it." He wasn't wrong. After my little mishap this morning, we went back to the square, had ice cream, then hopped on a water bus and visited an island on the other side of Venice. Lido was a beachside suburb full of quaint buildings and avenues lined with mature trees. We couldn't really make out where the sand met the water at the beach because of the mist or fog or whatever it was (I hoped it wasn't pollution), but still, it was a gorgeous place to stroll. After that, we visited the island of Saint Michele. It was a cemetery and creepy but interesting. A few famous bodies were buried there, including Ezra Pound and Stravinsky, so it attracted quite a few people. It was certainly more crowded than I'd expected. Apparently, Napoleon established the cemetery. So much history. Another reminder of what Australia lacked. I still loved my birth home, but I really loved my new one too.

"Good night. We have another big day tomorrow. I can't wait to see the glass-blowing."

Will turned on his side and pulled me in for a cuddle. "Yep, Angelica expects us at breakfast by eight."

I groaned. "I know. I was so hoping for some sleep-ins while we were here."

He laughed. "Eight *is* sleeping in. I swear, if sleeping were a sport, you'd be a gold medallist."

"I try to excel at everything I do."

"And you do." He waggled his brows and kissed me. Hmm, maybe we wouldn't be going to sleep straight away after all. He slid his lips to my neck. *Mmm, nice.*

A shrill scream took an ice pick to the peaceful night.

I started, and my eyelids flung open. Will and I launched out of bed, ready for action. Although, we couldn't exactly run downstairs with no clothes on. *Oops.* Will beat me to magicking clothes on, but I wasn't far behind. I ran to the window to look into the courtyard.

Two wall sconces threw dim light on the chairs and tables. The light barely reached a far corner of the courtyard, but it was enough to give an outline of two people, one of whom was sobbing and saying, "No, no, no. *Mio Dio,* no."

"What's she saying?" I really needed to learn other languages.

"My Italian isn't great, but I know that one. 'My god.' Let's get down there."

As I turned from the window, someone entered the court-yard, but I didn't have time to see who it was because Will grabbed my hand and pulled me towards the door. I snatched our key off the small table that sat against the wall. I grinned, proud of myself. How often did I remember to do practical things in an emergency... well, okay, even when it wasn't an emergency, I probably would've forgotten the key.

Will opened the door and dropped my hand, likely so we could run properly. We sprinted the whole way along the hall and downstairs, and I only just avoided slipping on the steep treads. I slowed and put up a return to sender, readying to grab my magic for anything. At the bottom of the stairs, we bolted to the right and through the door we'd gone in earlier that day. We burst into the courtyard, and Will's magic tingled my scalp. A ball of light appeared above one of the table umbrellas, illuminating the whole space.

"Good thinking, ninety-nine."

"Wouldn't I be Maxwell Smart? I'm the man, in case you hadn't noticed."

I smirked. "Oh, I've noticed. Anyway, it's just a saying." The end of the conversation and we'd reached the people in the corner. Of course, Angelica, Imani, and my mother were already there. They must've been who I glimpsed as I was leaving. My mother had her arm around a woman... the same woman who had argued with that guy this afternoon. The woman was crying and gesturing to a glass statue. Huh? That hadn't been there earlier today. Had it been cracked during delivery and she'd only just figured it out?

I looked past her and my mother at Imani and Angelica, who were giving the statue the once over. It was a life-size glass sculpture of a man. The head was blue, which faded into green, then yellow, then the legs were cream. For glass, the detail was incredible. I cocked my head to the side. It looked familiar. Was it stolen? Although why that lady would be so upset about it, I had no idea. Maybe she was worried about being accused of taking it?

Angelica finished inspecting the sculpture and spoke to the woman in Italian. After a bit of back and forth, Angelica nodded. She turned to Imani. "Record those three magic signatures and send them through to James. We'll see if they're on the system."

"Can you access international records?" I asked. For some stupid reason, I figured they usually accessed information on British people, but, of course, all the agencies would file their information into the PIB database, giving access to Paris, New York, Rome, and all the places that had bureaus. Embarrassment about my stupidity squashed the pride of remembering the keys. One cancelled out the other. Oh well.

Imani looked at me and raised her brow. "Lily, how long have you been working with us? I'm pretty sure you already know the answer to that."

I nodded and pressed my lips together. "Mmhmm. Yes. Yes, I do. Forget I said anything. Is it solid glass? It looks heavy." It would've taken some serious magic to move it here.

I walked past the woman and Angelica and placed my hand on the statue's shoulder. I loved the smooth coolness of glass. I wrinkled my forehead. "Oh. Is it warm because the weather's warm?"

Angelica donned her poker face. Oh dear. Why did she have to do that? Was the holiday over already? "It's warm because the man underneath it hasn't been dead for very long."

I snatched my hand back, my heart racing, and stared at the statue. "There's a real man under here?" Why did murder have to find us wherever we went?

"Yes, sort of. Someone turned him to glass, although his internal organs would still be there. His skin and hair, all the externals, have been turned to glass."

Will came to stand next to me. He scrutinised the face. "This is the man we saw this morning after your bird altercation."

My mouth dropped open. "It is too!" I didn't want to cast aspersions, but I turned and looked at the grieving woman, assessing her reaction. She did look pretty upset. A tissue was clutched in her fist, and her red eyes were still leaking tears. I put my hand on my stomach. Why was I feeling queasy? Maybe I'd had enough of crime and murder to last me forever. This was supposed to be time to escape, yet trouble always found us.

Angelica looked at Will. "I'll need to talk to both of you, but before I do, I want to check in with the local PIB. We've got two agents located in Trieste, a port city a couple of hours away. I don't want to lead this investigation because *a*, we're on holiday and *b*, I don't want Chad getting involved and messing anything up. I don't want to get the locals offside. Best let them lead this one. We can help if required."

Will and I shared a look of disbelief. Angelica taking a back seat? That was new. I pushed my unease aside and whispered to him, "Want to bet on it?" Maybe being silly would distract me until we could go back to bed and look forward to what we were doing tomorrow.

"Okay. I'm saying twenty-four hours."

"I'm saying twelve."

"What are the stakes?" Imani had approached. "I might want in."

I shrugged. "Fifty pounds?" I could afford that, and it was a large enough amount that the winner would get excited.

She grinned. "I'm in. I'm saying thirty hours."

I gave her an "are you kidding" look. "You sure?"

"She *is* on holidays. It might take a while for it to get the better of her." Imani smirked.

Angelica folded her arms. "I'll take this bet. I'm betting never."

We all stared at her. Will smiled. "Do you even know yourself?"

She smirked. "Better than anyone else does." She created a bubble of silence. "Lily, I don't want you taking any photos. This isn't important enough to risk your secret getting out, and we're on holidays. I also don't think the Italians would appreciate too much interference. We'll let them do their investigation their way. I'll offer to help, but I want you and Will to just enjoy the holiday." My whole body relaxed—we didn't have to get involved. Thank God. She waved us away and dropped the bubble of silence. "Go to bed. I'll deal with the law enforcement when they get here. They can figure this out. We're going to see the glass-blowing tomorrow. I still want you at breakfast at eight, so we can all enjoy each other's company." She looked at my mother, who'd been quiet this whole time. Did the crime bring back her own suffering and make her think of being imprisoned by Dana's father? Surely it must. "You can stay. You've always had a good eye for these things. We'll go up to the room shortly."

My mother gave her a small smile. "Thanks. This one's… interesting. It's been a long time." I figured Angelica was giving her an out in case she didn't want to go to the room by herself. I kept my sigh to myself—seeing my mum still tormented made my heart sore.

I slid my arms around Mum and kissed her cheek. "Night, Mum. See you tomorrow."

She squeezed me tight. "Night, my beautiful girl. Sweet dreams."

Will, Imani, and I made our way back inside. Even though I'd lose fifty pounds, I hoped that Angelica won the bet. I'd be so upset if our holiday was already all but over. Seriously, what did a girl have to do around here to get a break? At least Angelica hadn't asked me to take any photos. Maybe she was trying to spare me the grief on my holiday, or maybe she didn't want to offend the local agents? Whatever the reason, I was happy not to be involved. I was here to relax, and getting involved in a murder investigation wasn't high on anyone's list of relaxing things to do on holiday. Now I just had to hope the Italian authorities solved this one quickly.

The next morning, we woke at seven thirty to voices coming from the courtyard through the open window. A glimpse outside showed two men—witches—and Angelica. The men must be from the PIB. The statue was still there. Were they going to leave that poor man there forever? Surely not. It wasn't worth worrying about, though... well, as long as Angelica was coming to Murano—the island where the glass-blowing was—with us.

Thankfully, Angelica made it to breakfast, and then she came with us. Imani, Will, and I shared a surprised look as we left the hotel. I checked my watch. Only two-and-a-half more hours, and I'd lose the bet. Damn... sort of. There was also a yay that our holiday was still on track.

The boat trip to Murano was uneventful. I'd brought my Nikon, and I snapped a few shots along the way, including ones of my friends and family enjoying the ride. I even captured my mother's radiant smile a couple of times. Since we'd saved her, she hadn't been withdrawn, exactly, but whenever no one was talking to her, a faraway look glazed her eyes, and she sat expressionless. There must be so much going on in her head. I'd asked her a few times if she wanted to talk about it, but she refused. Maybe she just needed time to process. Goodness knew it had taken long enough for me to adjust to life in another country, and that wasn't nearly as stressful as being held captive for ten years and losing your husband. Oh, and also losing your magic. Sadness leeched into my heart, and I sighed.

Will, who was sitting next to me holding my hand, wrinkled his brow. "What's wrong?"

I blinked. "Oh, nothing. Just thinking about Mum." I gave him a sad smile.

He squeezed my hand. "I know. It'll get better slowly. You need to give her time. She'll find her way through it. Don't forget, she was an agent, and she survived this long. She's more resilient than you know."

"I suppose you're right." The boat slowed as we approached our stop. I pushed thoughts of my mother aside— I'd waited so long for this holiday, and I was going to do the best to enjoy it. Plus, Mum was here, which was way more than I'd expected. I smiled. "We're here!"

"Smile!" Imani pointed her phone at Will and me. I wasn't in many pictures because I was usually the one taking them, so I leaned into Will and did as asked. "You two are so cute." After a moment, she lowered the phone and looked at the screen. "I'll text them to you."

My phone pinged. "Thank you, lovely." I opened the app and showed Will. "Aw, look at us."

He grinned. "We look happy."

"We do." Warmth spread through my chest. I was actually

in Venice, on the trip of a lifetime with the man of my dreams. So many cliches, but so good.

Lavender, who'd been sitting opposite us, folded his arms. "When am I going to get you on the runway, William? You'd kill it."

Will adopted a no-nonsense expression. "Never, Lav. My sister is the model in this family, and that's fine with me."

Sarah laughed. "Lav's right. You'd rake it in. But I'm not encouraging you. Having my big brother around all the time would be… suffocating."

I shook my head. "Lav, you can't have him. If he's swanning around with a whole lot of gorgeous models, he'll probably leave me, and then I'll blame you, and we won't be able to be friends."

"Lovie, Will knows what he's got. I don't think any of those ladies would be enough to tempt him." Maybe Lavender was right, but maybe he wasn't, and I didn't want to take that chance.

Will bumped his shoulder against mine. "Don't worry, Lily. You've got me forever, and I am never modelling anything." He picked up my hand and waved it around. "This ring proves it." I was being so stupid, but I couldn't help it. Since we'd rescued my mother and shut down RP, I was waiting for something to go wrong. We'd never had proper peace. I could even wander up to Costa by myself or just with Liv and have a meal without worrying someone would kill me. It was a novel experience for sure. But how long would it last? The watercraft shuddered to a halt, interrupting my waste-of-time-and-energy thoughts.

The water bus docked, and we stood. We filed off onto Murano and followed Angelica. She might not be leading the investigation, but she was leading our expedition. Whatever made her happy was fine with me. Not having to organise stuff made my life easier.

The cobbled path had lagoon on one side and a brick wall and buildings on the other. The sun shone and sparkled off the water, and a crowd of tourists ambled along the pathway. We couldn't have asked for nicer weather.

We passed a factory-looking building with a front court-yard behind the tall brick fence and iron gates. It advertised glass-blowing demonstrations for five euros a person. "Why aren't we stopping here?"

"She probably knows somewhere better," said Imani.

"Of course she does." I should know not to ask. Angelica had a reason for everything. Maybe she was friends with whoever we were going to visit? It wouldn't surprise me—she had connections everywhere.

We bypassed another glass-blowing place that had demon-strations advertised for four euros. We finally stopped at a third. I narrowed my eyes. The building looked similar to the others we'd passed. "This one's ten euros a visitor."

Will looked at me. "Since when did you become a cheapskate?"

"I'm not. I'm just wondering. Maybe they're better than the others?"

"What do you mean, love?" Imani asked as we followed Angelica through the front courtyard and to the door.

"The others were way cheaper than this. It's probably because this one's the best. I'm sure there's a reason we're here and not there." I shrugged. Will and Imani shared a *look*. I raised a brow and lowered my voice. "Do you think this is part of the investigation?" The guy had been turned to glass after all. Maybe a glass-blowing professional had a vendetta against the victim?

Imani shrugged. "She could still be questioning someone even if she wasn't giving up her holiday and leading the investigation."

"How are we supposed to find out?" Gah! I should've spent time listening in on her conversation with those agents. They hadn't used a bubble of silence. Oh, but they'd been speaking in Italian. I really was in holiday mode. And who could blame me? I'd spent over twelve months in constant panic mode. Now my brain was like, oh, a crime? I can't hear you. La, la, la, la, la.

Liv, who was in front of me with Beren, stopped walking and turned to me. "Just chill, lady. Enjoy the holiday. Angelica's going to let those agents handle this, and you should too. Don't give it a second thought."

Will nodded. "Listen to Liv. We're here to see the sights. It's not our circus, not our monkeys."

Angelica turned to Will and smiled. "Will's right. Now, who's ready to watch some artisans at work?" She turned away from us before we answered, then addressed a young woman who'd approached her. Angelica went with the woman to the cash register and took out her credit card.

"She can't pay for everyone!" I stepped forward to pay for Will and myself, but Will grabbed my wrist, stopping me.

"Don't worry. She can afford it, and I'm pretty sure she wants to. We'll buy her a drink later."

I gave up. "Okay." It was nice of her, but I hated owing people things. I was more than happy to pay for her, but not the other way around. Yes, it was hypocritical, but that was how I rolled. Fending for myself over the years had made me self-reliant. Asking for favours went against the grain, and Angelica had done so much for me already—letting me live in her home rent-free and risking her life to help find out what happened to my parents. I could hardly ask for more.

While Angelica chatted to the woman serving her, I wandered around the showroom. So many gorgeous things. Multi-coloured sea creatures—fish, octopus, and starfish— lined the shelves. There were glasses and goblets, and, um, look at those prices. It was cool if you wanted one glass, but to get a set would cost a fortune. And then I'd be too scared to use them in case I smashed one. Ooh, pussy cats. Oh my God! Was that a tiny squirrel? The little squirrel standing on his hind legs was about an inch high. Orange, blue, yellow, and black swathes of colour swept from his feet to his head and the tip of his tail. His little friend next to him was on all fours, its tail high in the air. They were only ten euros each. I picked them up, just in case someone else grabbed them.

Amusement laced Imani's voice. "Oh, what a surprise that you picked those."

I grinned. "I know, right? You gotta admit; they're super cute."

Will shook his head. "Tree rats are not cute."

I swatted his arm. "Don't be mean. They're adorable." I went to the counter and paid just as Angelica finished up and turned around.

"Our demonstration starts in two minutes. Come this way." She and my mother led the way through a door at the side of the shop and straight into a high-clearance, concrete-floored area. The bare brick walls and exposed ceiling beams had oodles of character. I wondered how old this place was. Had it always been a glass factory? I could imagine a smithy making horseshoes and swords… proper metal ones, not glass ones.

A large white sign had pictures of a black phone, a

camera, and a video camera with red circles and lines through them. No photos. How ridiculous. Grrrrr. I'd come all this way, and we'd paid, and we couldn't have a reminder of our visit. Well, I guessed the reminder would be the trinkets the tourists bought. It still irked me. I took a deep breath and let out the angst. I was still here experiencing it, so I'd be grateful for that. Every day was precious, and I'd do well to remember it. Enjoy things for what they were and not get caught up wishing they were something else.

Two rows of bench seats set up like mini-bleachers sat along a wall to our left. A furnace sat in the middle of the room; two artisans dressed in jeans and T-shirts stood near it. I blinked. They weren't wearing aprons or gloves. As Will and I took our seats in the front, and Sarah and Lav sat to the other side of me, I whispered to Will, "Surely protective gear would be sensible?"

"They're witches. They'll be fine. Even the non-witch artisans don't wear them. I guess they have years of experience and don't need them?"

The lady who'd sold the tickets to Angelica, stood just in front of the seats and to the left. Her English was excellent, as was her melodious Italian accent. "Good morning, everyone. Welcome to Zanini Murano glass factory. Today, Francesco Zanini will demonstrate the exquisite art of glass-blowing, which started in Venice in around the seventh to eight centuries before Christ."

Francesco held a long metal pole. He rolled the end of it in glass beads, stuck the pole into the fire, then took it out and started his work, all the while the woman explaining what he was doing. When he blew into the pole, the real magic started. The glass expanded. Francesco twisted the pole, then blew a bit more. He worked the glass with tongs too. At the end, he'd created a small giraffe. I shook my head. Pretty amazing. He then started another piece, which ended up being part of a light fitting, and I didn't feel any magic whatsoever. He wasn't even using his witch powers. Impressive.

After twenty minutes, the show was over. We all filed out… except for Angelica and my mother, who stayed to chat with Francesco. The rest of us perused the shop, and I pulled out my camera to take photos of the cute glass art. I wouldn't mind getting a couple more things for myself before we left Venice, and I also wanted to grab a present for Millicent and my gorgeous niece. There were plenty of shops that sold this stuff near where we were staying, so I could always go there later. The photos would also help me compare prices because who wanted to pay top dollar?

The most gorgeous, life-size chubby sparrow sat on a shelf. I bent forward and peered closer. It was so detailed. Surely they'd done this one with magic. How else could they render each feather so precisely? It was three hundred and forty-nine euros—worth every euro cent, but too expensive for me. I'd have to console myself with a photo. I lifted my phone and snapped a shot, then froze. I blinked. That couldn't be right. I lifted my phone again. Through the viewfinder was the glass sculpture, but when I clicked and captured the shot, there was a real sparrow. Liv was standing nearby, checking out a cat-sized dolphin. "Hey, tell me what you see." I handed her the phone.

"Looks like a sparrow to me."

"A real one, or a glass one?"

She wrinkled her forehead. "A real one." She zoomed into the shot. "Yes, definitely real."

"That's what I thought. It's a picture of that." I took my phone back and nodded at the clear, blue, and brown glass sparrow on the shelf. It was kind of like that man today. Not that I'd taken a photo of him, but it was a real bird turned to glass, which was why it probably looked so real. That poor bird. I frowned.

Liv sucked in a breath and gently picked it up. She turned it around, studying it. "You'd never know. Do you think they killed it first or spelled it alive?"

Poor birdie. "I have no idea. Hopefully they stopped its heart before they performed the spell. How horrific if it suffocated to death."

"What are you two going on about?" Beren stood next to Liv. She explained and handed the bird to him. He checked it out, then looked at me. "Show me the photo." I held the phone up for him to see. He pressed his lips together and looked back and forth between the real bird and the photo. "Right." He turned and took the bird to the counter.

The blood drained from my face, and dizziness hit me. "He's not going to say something, is he? He can't out my secret."

I ran after him. As he reached the register, I grabbed his arm. "B, you can't say anything."

He looked at me, his expression calm. "Don't worry. I'm not that stupid, Lily. I'm going to buy it. We can study it back at the hotel."

Cool relief doused my panic. "Oh, okay. Just making sure."

He gave me a lopsided smile. "Your secret is always going to be safe with me." Of course it was. I was stupid for thinking otherwise.

"Thanks. Um… you're going to spend that much money?"

"Yep. Don't worry. I can afford it, and if it ties into the case, the PIB will reimburse me." I should've known he had it all figured out.

Magic I didn't recognise feathered my scalp. Beren and I looked at each other before gazing around the shop. No one was glowing. I turned back to B. "Must be in the workshop. Come to think of it, Mum and Angelica are still in there." I narrowed my eyes. "You don't think they're investigating, do you?"

"I wondered why Angelica picked this particular factory."

A young lady approached the register. "Can I help you?"

Beren handed her the sparrow. "I'd like to buy this, please." While she rang up the sale, I watched the door to the glass-blowing area. After a few seconds, Mum and Angelica walked through. What had they been up to? Angelica's poker face gave nothing away, and my mother's face was relaxed, as if she were on holiday. Looked like she was poker-facing in a different way. They were all such professionals. Me, on the other hand….

Angelica smiled at me. "What's wrong, dear?" Exhibit *A* for crap poker face.

"Ah, nothing. Just wondering what happened to you two."

Angelica's serene face bugged me. I would bet she was hiding something. Oh, hang on… I *did* bet, but because of her poker face and secrecy, I was going to lose. I only had myself to blame. No one forced me to bet. Let's hope I learned my lesson. "I've always been fascinated about the art, and Francesco was only too happy to tell us more about it."

"You haven't taken over the case, have you?" I checked the time on my phone. I had about thirty minutes left before I lost. Could I get her to admit she was leading the investigation?

"Of course not. I'm enjoying my holiday. Now, if you don't mind, I'd like to peruse the wares." Angelica wandered off, but my mother stayed.

"That was fascinating, wasn't it?"

I smiled. "It sure was. Totally worth the wait. Are you going to buy anything?"

"I'm not sure. Maybe not here. I might look around when we get back to the main island." She turned her head to the left and right, surveying the room.

"What's wrong?"

She gave me a fake smile. I'd had so many years without her, but I still remembered what that looked like. "Nothing, sweetie. I'm fine. Let's look around." She linked her arm through mine and pulled me towards the displays.

She wasn't fooling me that easily. "We're safe here. Dana and her dad are both dead."

Mum didn't look at me, but she nodded. "Oh, look. Isn't this a gorgeous fish?"

Changing the subject. I guessed she didn't want to talk about it, and that was okay. She'd pushed through her fears and probably PTSD and come on holiday with us. The least I could do was accept that she was going to be jumpy and overly cautious. Even I couldn't avoid looking around and behind me constantly when I was in Westerham. "Yes, it's lovely."

We'd heal eventually—it was just going to take time. And, thankfully, we finally had plenty of that.

CHAPTER 4

I breathed in through my nose and shut my eyes. Oh my God, it was so good. The garlic aroma sent my tastebuds into overdrive, and they drenched my mouth. We'd ordered our food at a pizza place near our hotel, and waiting was torture. We sat around the table in the noisy restaurant. It was hard to talk to anyone who wasn't right next to you, which meant I could only chat to Will and Imani. My mum sat across from me, in between Angelica and Liv. Beren sat next to Liv, and Sarah and Lavender sat on each table end, Sarah closest to her brother and Lav on the end near Imani. Everyone seemed to be having a good time, laughing and talking, even my mum. *Suck it, Piranha. I got my mother back, and you're dead, so there.* I was going to have to stop thinking about the evil witch eventually, but I figured I was allowed to have a few months of gloating quietly.

Imani leaned close to me. "How does it feel to lose?"

My twelve hours had come and gone, and if we couldn't prove Angelica was heading up the investigation in the next few hours, Will would lose too. "Whatever. I wouldn't be surprised if I'd actually won. If Angelica doesn't give herself up, how will we ever know?"

"Are you saying we were stupid for betting on it?"

"Possibly. So, has she been telling you anything about the case? Did you get the results on those magic signatures?" I wasn't that worried about solving the crime because I didn't think it was a serial-killer sort of thing. The guy had probably been targeted because he'd upset someone.

"Two of them aren't in the system, but one was. A man with links to the mafia. He's done time, but he's been out of trouble for the past seven years."

"He wouldn't happen to work at the glass-blowing factory we visited today."

Imani pressed her lips together. "I don't know. I wasn't given that information."

"I bet he does, otherwise, why did we visit that particular one? Plus, Angelica and my mother stayed back in the demonstration room for quite a while after we came out."

Angelica's magic feathered my scalp, and she stared at me. "What did I do?" She used a small amount of magic to project her voice to Imani and me. Of course she'd heard me even though I'd been speaking as quietly as possible close to Imani's ear.

"Just wondering why we went to that particular glass-blowing factory. Does one of the suspects work there?" There was no point pretending I didn't say anything. She always knew what was going on.

"Yes, he does. But he had an alibi that checks out. Now, no more work talk. We're on holidays." She looked to her left as a waiter arrived with garlic bread. He placed one of the bread-baskets in the middle and then set one near each end of the table. "Looks like it's time to eat." She smiled. Whether she was happy about not having to tell me anything else or about the food being here, who could say?

I couldn't believe they would just take the alibi as gold. Most people had someone who would be happy to lie for them, and unless Angelica had cast a truth spell—which was illegal except in certain circumstances which didn't apply here —she couldn't know for sure. If James was here, he'd be able to tell. Had Angelica checked whether the guy had motive?

Will nudged my arm with his. "Here, have some garlic bread, and stop thinking about the case."

I took two pieces from the basket and passed it to Imani. "Sorry. I can't help it."

He grinned. "Are you sure you don't want to become an agent?"

"I'm sure." He had a good point though. If I didn't want to be an agent, why did I care? I wanted to be a photographer, so I should be out there taking photos. Fine. Tomorrow morning, I was going to get up early, at sunrise, and go take some early morning pictures when the light was magical.

The rest of our dinner arrived. I shut my eyes and savoured the delicious scent of my anchovy pizza. I opened my eyes to Will and Imani pulling disgusted faces at me. "What?"

Imani shook her head. "I don't know how you can eat that stinking fish."

Will shuddered. "No kissing me until you've brushed your teeth."

I rolled my eyes. "Tease me all you want. At least I never have to share." I grinned. "Yum!" I took a bite and groaned. Talk about heaven. "Mmmmmmm." Will and Imani shared a "vomit" look. I didn't really want to give away even one anchovy, but I couldn't resist. Imani had twisted her spaghetti bolognaise onto her fork and lifted it to her mouth. Just as she was about to put it in, I drew a smidge of magic and transferred one of the anchovies from my pizza onto her fork. In her mouth it went. She started chewing, then stopped. Her eyes widened. She grabbed her napkin, lifted it to her mouth, and spat her food into it. I laughed.

Angelica's voice carried across the table… without magic. "What inappropriate public behaviour, Imani. Are you trying to embarrass me?"

I snorted. Imani pinched her lips together and turned to me. "You!"

I grinned and shrugged. I wasn't going to admit to anything. Besides, Will was only watching and didn't know what had happened. I was going to get him too. "Me? I didn't do anything."

Angelica shook her head and went back to her food and whatever my mother was saying.

Imani leaned towards me. "I felt your magic."

"I was removing some food I'd dropped on my shirt. You know how clumsy I am."

She narrowed her eyes at me, then peered at the masticated food in her napkin.

I wrinkled my brow. My acting game needed to be on point. "What are you doing?"

"Looking for that damn anchovy."

I activated my best surprised face. "Did they accidentally put one in your food?"

She puckered her lips. "It wasn't a *they*; it was a *you*." The urge to giggle was strong, so I shoved my pizza into my mouth and took a bite. When I was done with that mouthful, I subtly looked at Will. He was eating a pepperoni pizza. The flavour was pretty strong, so he'd be less likely to notice any anchovies. I'd have to wait until he had more of his garlic bread. Luckily, I didn't have long to wait. As it was about to go in his mouth, I plonked two of my anchovy pieces onto it. In it went.

His face twisted in horror, and he slammed his napkin over his mouth and coughed. Angelica stared at him and raised a brow as if to say, not you too. "I can't take you lot anywhere." She pinned her school-teacher gaze on me. "Lily, stop behaving like an adolescent."

I burst out laughing. Revenge was sweet. "They started it."

My mother shook her head and laughed. "That's the Lily I remember. Always so cheeky."

I smiled at her. "I try."

Angelica turned to my mother. "How am I supposed to keep her in line if you don't back me up?"

"Good luck with that. I tried for fourteen years, and she's still the same three-year-old who put a dead lizard in her brother's sandwich after he broke one of her dolls, and still the same twelve-year-old who hid her father's car keys after he punished her for something her brother did. He couldn't find them for two days." She shook her head. "He was so angry. She didn't admit to taking them until he apologised for wrongly punishing her, but he still grounded her afterwards for hiding his keys. Those were good times."

"Getting grounded was not good times, Mum. But having Dad around was." I gave her a sad smile, which she returned. "Sorry I gave you grief as a kid."

"You weren't any worse than any other child. I'm glad you had some fight in you, Lily. From what Angelica says, it's helped get you through everything."

I didn't hear it, but Angelica's phone must have rung because she pulled it out of her bag and answered it. "Hello,

Angelica DuPree speaking." She listened for a moment, then said something in Italian. Hmm, interesting.

I turned to Will. "Do you think that's the Italian PIB guy?"

"I have no idea. And for the record, when you least expect it, expect it."

"You were mean to me first."

"We were just teasing."

"So was I."

"But it was *anchovy*." He shuddered again.

"Poor baby. Did you have a drink to wash out the taste?"

"Yes."

"Can you still taste it?"

"No, but that's not th—"

"Yes it is. You suffered for approximately five seconds. Time to get over it." I smiled.

Angelica's magic tickled my scalp. Her voice easily reached me, and I suspected everyone else at our table. "I'm sorry, everyone, but I have to go. I'll see you all for a nightcap later at the hotel."

"Where are you going?" I asked.

"That's on a need-to-know basis, dear." She stood. "Enjoy your dinner." Angelica slung her handbag over her shoulder and left.

Imani spoke over my head to Will. "I wonder if we should be paying you out the bet."

"There's only one way to find out. We should follow her, but I don't want to. We've come here for a holiday, and she knows that. I don't want to leave in the middle of a meal to maybe win two hundred pounds." He grabbed my hand. "As much as I hated that mouthful of anchovy, I came here to enjoy my fiancée's company. We've been through a ridiculous amount of pain to finally be able to enjoy ourselves. I'm not missing a minute."

"Well said." Sarah smiled from her spot at the end of the table. "We'll just ask her about it later. She did say she'd be back for a nightcap. Besides, Lav and I have to go to work tomorrow morning. Apparently the forecast has changed, and it's supposed to be good weather."

I frowned. "Bummer."

Lavender nodded. "And I was looking forward to shopping. We're hoping to be back late tomorrow afternoon. Anyone care to come with?"

I looked at Will. He shook his head. "No thanks. I hate shopping."

I turned to Imani. "I hate shopping, too, love. I'm sure I have some reading I want to catch up on. I don't get much time to do that when I'm on call."

I shrugged. "I'll come. It'll be fun to hang out with you two for a couple of hours."

With that decided, we chatted about random stuff and finished our meal. When we returned to the hotel, Beren and Liv went upstairs, and the rest of us retired to the quaint bar area. It was a dimly lit room, which contained a grand piano, small bar, and clusters of couches with coffee tables. An ostentatious chandelier hung in the middle of the room. Based on what the small Venetian-glass things cost, that must have been worth in the five figures.

There was only one other couple in the bar area and a young man sitting by himself. It wasn't easy in the low light, but I recognised that he was the porter who magicked our bags to our rooms when we arrived. He sat slumped on a couch, a drink in one hand and a scowl on his face. Every now and then, his glare flicked to the bartender. Interesting. Looked like someone had a bad day. Had these colleagues had an argument? I shook my head. *Stop worrying about other people and relax.*

We found Angelica sitting on a couch against the far wall, a glass of what looked like white wine in her hand. As Will, Imani, and I sat on one lounge, Sarah and Lavender sat on another, and my mum plonked next to Angelica. "What does everyone want to drink?" asked Will. We gave him our orders, and he went to the bar.

I leaned forward and looked at Angelica. "What's the latest on the crime?" At least it wasn't too loud in here, some jazz music playing softly in the background. So much easier to be heard than the restaurant.

Angelica made a bubble of silence. "Do you really want to know? I thought you were on holiday?"

I couldn't help asking because I hated not knowing stuff, not to mention, we had a bet riding on it. "I am, but I'm curious. Besides, you took us to that glass-blowing factory for a reason, and I'm sure it was only because it was related to the crime. I'm pretty sure you're on holiday too."

"She has you there." Mum chuckled. It was nice to have someone backing me up against Angelica. My mum was definitely brave.

"Hmm, yes, well." Angelica glanced towards the bar. "Let's wait for Will to come back before we start." Thankfully, he wasn't long, returning with a large tray of drinks. Once they were distributed, he sat, and Angelica resumed. "We traced one of the magic signatures to a criminal, the glass-blowing artisan from today, Lorenzo. He's been clean for a few years, as in the police haven't caught him doing anything. Anyway, he had an alibi that checked out, but the call I got earlier was Matteo from the Italian PIB. They've found a motive. The Dal Lago family—the owners of this lovely hotel

—owe Lorenzo's company over two hundred thousand euros. He's been trying to get his money for the past six months, but they won't pay."

I gazed around the uncrowded room. "What do the rest of the hotel's finances look like? It doesn't seem to be overrun with tourists, and it's the busy time of year."

Lavender sipped his cocktail, then placed it back on the table. "Yes, but if you're only catering to witches, you've probably reduced your potential clientele to one in ten or less. We don't exactly make up a lot of the population."

"That sparrow I found, the one Beren bought, did you send it for testing?"

"Yes, dear. It's as you thought—a real sparrow turned to glass, the same as our victim, Antonio Dal Lago. The glassblower is obviously our strongest lead right now, but the fact that his alibi checks out—he was at his niece's birthday party —leaves us without a clear-cut case."

"But why was his magic signature on the victim?" my mother asked.

"Lorenzo says it's because he made him promise under oath to repay the loan in thirty days. Lorenzo cast the oath spell. He showed us video footage of Antonio coming to the office at the factory the day before the transformation happened." Angelica finished off the wine in her glass.

Will leaned forward and sat on the edge of the couch. "What about that woman he was arguing with that afternoon? How is she related to him?"

"That's his wife," Angelica answered.

Will picked up his glass and moved it so the liquid and ice swirled around. "Do you know what they were fighting about?"

"No. She claimed she was too upset to talk to us."

I raised a brow. "For someone who isn't leading the investigation, you sure know a lot."

She cocked her head to the side but didn't say anything in answer to that particular comment. "We've hit a dead end, which means we'll have to start questioning the rest of the staff here. The Italian agents have said I can sit in when they're interviewing tomorrow."

"Can you check for magic signatures around here in the meantime? If it was someone who works here, we'll know soon enough." Since it was a hotel catering to witches, they'd use their magic whenever they felt like it. "Surely no one would change a bed manually when they could magic it. Putting that fitted sheet on is a b—."

"We don't have cause to do that yet, Lily. You should know better. Until we can figure out a potential motive, we're not allowed to search anything."

"But who would even know? Can't you look for them and check them against the ones you found? At least you'll know whether to push harder or forget about it."

Angelica sighed. "What if the culprit does work here but their signature isn't even on the body? Then we'll give up before we should. Your idea is terrible, dear. Also, we could do it that way, but it's an invasion of privacy. It's like sneakily checking out someone's diary or their medicine cabinet. It just isn't done. Bad etiquette, dear."

"Good etiquette isn't Lily's strong suit." Will smirked.

"I'm not that bad. Sheesh. It's not like I chew with my mouth open."

Angelica raised a brow. "And I suppose allowing tree rats to sit and eat on my kitchen table is the height of polite behaviour?"

"They're not rats! Anyway, rats are cute." Bagel and

WESTERHAM WITCHES AND A VENETIAN VENDETTA

Cinnamon came to mind. They'd been rather helpful when it came to cracking the RP investigation, and they were clever and polite. "It's not like I do it when you're eating there. And I always clean up afterwards."

"Knowing a squirrel has defecated on my kitchen table is not comforting in the least... whether or not you cleaned up afterwards. I suggest you entertain them outside from now on, as you did this morning." Angelica's serious gaze brooked no argument, but my mum pressed her lips together. Was she trying not to laugh?

Gah, this was so silly, and Angelica was such a party pooper. I sighed. "Okay." As much as I hated this turn of events, it was her table and her home, so I wasn't going to argue about where I hung out with my squirrels. If she wanted us outside, I'd respect her wishes. At least now I could do things outdoors whenever I wanted and not worry about being attacked. Will and I could probably get our own place together, but now my mum had moved in, there was no way I wanted to move out. We had a ridiculous amount of catching up and spending time together to do.

I couldn't believe they were giving up on that glass-blower so quickly. "Even though that glass-blower guy had an alibi, it could still be him, surely. They must have other glass-blowers on staff too. Maybe it was one of them? I mean, that sparrow ended up just like Antonio."

Imani drained her glass. "They're not giving up on him... just looking for more clues." She turned to Angelica. "They had money problems and were seen arguing. Surely we have grounds to suspect the wife and take her magic signature?"

"Possibly. The Italians aren't as quick to jump to those conclusions. After you told me about their fight, I spoke to our Italian agents, and they explained that since they're such a passionate bunch and frequently raise their voices and gesticulate to make their point that they might not have been having a serious argument."

Were they kidding? "It looked pretty serious to me." Will blew out a breath. I felt his pain. If only one of us knew Italian. "We couldn't understand what they were saying. They could've been arguing about him leaving his bathroom towel on the floor or the toilet seat up. If only Sarah, Angelica, or Mum had been there instead of us." Will narrowed his eyes at my assessment.

Imani laughed. "Yes, those arguments are sometimes the most heated. Although I don't think I've ever covered a murder where that was the reason."

I cocked my head to the side. "Maybe it was the proverbial straw?"

"It might have been, dear, but that conjecture is not enough to warrant asking for her MS." Ooh, Angelica was getting all short form on us. "The Italian agents have the lead on this, so we have to comply."

I sat back and slammed my shoulders into a cushion. "Why are we even bothering? This is our holiday. It's too complicated, and my brain could do without the worry."

"No one's forcing you to think about it, dear. I was happy to hand it over to the Italians, but they asked for my help, and I would never say no. They're short-staffed—just like the rest of the PIB." Of course she wouldn't say no. Angelica was a crime-fighting angel—her name said it all. Now I felt bad because I was turning my back on a dead man who probably hadn't deserved what he'd gotten. Plus, Angelica deserved a break too. Goodness knew she'd been through a lot in the last year. Although, maybe being on holiday wasn't her happy place. Maybe her super happy place was solving crimes? I was glad that Will wasn't that crazy in love with the job.

"I'm just worried that you need a break; that's all."

She smiled. "I am having a break. This is a low-stress case, and I'm sightseeing in between working things out. It's nice that you're thinking of me."

"I can't help it. I guess it's what I do." A woman walked up to the bar and slipped behind it to join the bartender. She stood in front of him and whispered in his ear. He smiled, slid his arm around her waist, and nuzzled her cheek with his nose. "That looks cosy."

Will furrowed his brow. "Isn't that Mrs Dal Lago?"

My eyes widened. "It is! I wasn't sure because it's so dark, but, yeah, that looks like her. Do you think she's having an affair?"

"Looks like it," said Imani.

"It might be time for me to grab another drink." Angelica stood and made her way to the bar. This should be interesting. We all watched as she did her thing, and we weren't the only ones. The young man on the couch, whose frown hadn't budged, looked even angrier if it was possible. What was the deal with that? Was Mrs Dal Lago having an affair with him too?

Lavender smirked. "What a busy woman. If she does admit to having an affair, will it be enough to grab her magic signature?"

Will shook his head. "I don't think so. More of a motive would be a large life insurance policy. Don't forget; the Italians are a passionate lot, according to our fellow agents."

I rolled my eyes. "That must get them out of a lot of fines and arrests. Oh, I'm so passionate about this glass bird, but I can't afford it, so I just lost my mind and took it."

Imani laughed. "What would be their excuse for speeding? They loved the sound of the engine?"

"Sounds about right." I chuckled. Angelica returned. "That was quick."

Her poker face was intact. "She readily admitted to it and said her husband knew. That's what they were fighting about, supposedly. She said they had an open marriage."

I blinked. "If the marriage was so open, why were they fighting about it?"

She sat back down. "Maybe she was lying? I'll have to dig deeper. But don't worry, it won't affect our holiday." Hmm, that would remain to be seen. Well, it wouldn't affect my holiday, but it might affect hers. People would do what they wanted, so I didn't bother saying anything. And it looked like that porter's glarefest was over. The elderly woman who'd welcomed us earlier came in and went straight to him. Her back was to me, so I couldn't see her expression, but whatever she said made the young man's scowl fade, and now he just looked sad. He stood, and they left together. Hmm, doubly interesting.

Lavender clapped, grabbing my attention. "Ready for shopping tomorrow? Sarah and I can't wait to introduce you to haute couture."

I gave him a "you've got to be kidding" look. "I can't afford that stuff. I'll only be able to say hello. There won't be any getting to know it better."

Sarah laughed. "You're hilarious. Just wait. You might just fall in love with something and have to have it."

"According to the Italian way of doing things, maybe I could just take it if I was passionate enough about it?"

Angelica shook her head. "Please don't get arrested, dear. It would make me look bad."

"Yes, because that's the first thing I'd worry about. The going-to-jail thing doesn't bother me at all." I grinned. Been there, done that. I didn't need another experience.

Someone's phone rang. Angelica was the one who fished it out of her bag. "Pronto. Sono Angelica." It must be the Italian agents. For something that wasn't supposed to intrude on our holiday, it sure was butting in. She said something else I couldn't understand, then hung up and stood. "We have another body that's been turned to glass—a woman. They want my expertise. I'll see you all tomorrow. Sorry to dash." She looked at my mother. "I should be back in the next couple of hours. Will you be okay, or do you want to come with me?"

My mother hesitated, likely thinking about it. She looked up and gave a nod. "I think I'll come with." She stood and came over to me.

I stood and gave her a hug and kiss on the cheek. "Goodnight, Mum. Stay safe."

"I'll be fine. It's rather exciting, actually, being back in the thick of it." She gave everyone a wave. "Night, all." They left.

Having Angelica getting caught up in this was one thing, but now my mother was ditching us too? I looked around at each of my friends. How long until we were all distracted and not on holiday anymore?

Turned out, not long at all.

CHAPTER 5

T he next morning I'd gotten up early and made my way to Saint Mark's Square. The ornate street lamps on poles were still shining because the sun wasn't really up. It was low in the sky, casting long, golden rays on the paving through the arches of the Doge Palace. A gilded veil swathed the cathedral, the walls seeming to glow with heavenly light. Only a couple of people were around, lending the peaceful morning a dreamlike quality.

I clicked off shot after shot with my Nikon, getting the square and buildings from all different angles. Before I knew it, the sun had risen further, and the light was losing its ethereal quality, brightening and flattening the images in process. The magic had evaporated, but the experience would bring me joy for a long time to come. I breathed in the warm, salty air and ignored the hint of sewerage odour in it. Nothing in life was perfect… except squirrels—I was pretty sure there wasn't anything I would change about them.

I made my way back to the hotel and went straight up to

the room to grab Will. We might as well have breakfast, then a wander around. There were a couple of stops I'd seen on the way back from Murano yesterday that I wanted to check out. When I opened the door, I stopped short. "Mum, good morning." I placed my camera on the table and gave her a hug. The hairs raised on my nape, and it had nothing to do with magic. My mum's face had looked worried just as I went in for the hug, and Will's poker face... well, that spoke volumes. I ended the hug and looked at Mum. "What's wrong?"

She glanced at Will, then looked back at me. "It's Angelica. We met with the Italian agents at the crime scene, and after about half an hour, I yawned—I'm not used to so much exercise and activity. Being locked in a cage most of the day really does a number on your fitness.... But, anyway, Angelica insisted I come back here and that she'd be back as soon as she could." Her cheeks reddened, and she looked at the ground. "I fell asleep waiting." Her gaze returned to mine. "When I woke up this morning, she wasn't here, and her bed hadn't been slept in. I would've felt if she'd spelled her bed neat—I can't cast spells, but I still feel it if someone else does. And she said we'd have breakfast together at seven thirty, which is in thirty minutes. If she wasn't coming, she would've called."

My forehead tightened. I lifted my hand to my mouth to bite my nail, but I forced it back down. I needed to hide my worry. Mum didn't need to see me stressing right now. Angelica had often disappeared in the last few months, so maybe she'd had something urgent to deal with? "Have you tried calling her?"

"Yes, early this morning, and so did Will just before you came. Her phone rings, then goes to voicemail."

Will lifted his phone. "I've just texted James to get the number for the Italian agents."

As much as Angelica could look after herself, I had a bad feeling about this. Hopefully our worry was misplaced, and she'd turn up any time now. Will's phone dinged. "I got James out of bed, but he's come through." Will tapped his phone screen and put it on speaker. "Hopefully they speak English."

"Pronto."

"Ah, hello. This is Agent Blakesley from the London PIB office. Do you speak English?"

"Yes, Agent Blakesley. I am Agent Enrico Tondato. What can I do for you?"

"I was wondering if I could speak to Agent DuPree. She's not answering her phone, and I know she was meeting with you last night. She hasn't returned."

Silence for a few moments, which was plenty of time for the hairs on my arms to follow the example of the ones on my nape and stand up. Finally, his Italian accent came through loud and clear. "She left us last night at about 1:00 a.m. to return to the 'otel."

"She never showed up." Will ran a hand through his hair, and my mother sat on the bed and clasped her hands together in her lap. After everything she'd been through, this was the last thing she needed. I sat next to her and placed my hand over hers.

"I'm sorry, but I don't know where she is. If you don't hear from her by midday, please let me know. I'm sorry, but I must go. Ciao."

Will's mouth was open, maybe to say goodbye, but the phone was dead. He shut his mouth and slid the phone into his pocket. "Katerina, can you take us to where you two were last night?"

Mum bit her bottom lip. "Yes, of course."

Will's poker face materialised. "She might have had some

urgent business to attend to. I know it's unlike her to not tell anyone, but maybe she thought she'd be quick. We'll check everything out just as a precaution." He looked at me. "Be prepared to take some pictures."

"Okay." I stood and grabbed my camera from the table. I could've used my phone, but at least I'd look super touristy with the Nikon. "Ready?"

"Yep. Let's go."

On the way down the hall, Will knocked on Beren and Liv's door and explained what had happened. "If you guys can stay close to here in case we need you to travel somewhere, that would be great. And if Angelica returns, you can give us a call."

Beren nodded. "Sounds like a plan. Good luck."

After we said goodbye, Will knocked on Imani's door and explained what happened. "Can you come with us?"

"Of course, love. Let's do this."

"Are you going to tell Sarah and Lav?" I asked.

"No. They would've already left for their photo shoot. There's no use stressing them out until we have more information."

He made sense, so I nodded and took a deep breath, trying to fill myself with air rather than worry.

We hurried out, Mum leading the way. Instead of turning left in the alleyways to head towards Saint Mark's Square, she turned right, and we speed walked through narrow passage after narrow passage between buildings, dodging crowds as we went. After a few minutes, I was thoroughly lost. What a rabbit warren. "You don't think those agents did something to her, do you?"

Imani, who was behind me, answered, "No. Why would they?"

"Maybe they didn't like her taking over their investigation?"

Will, who was in front of me, at my mother's heel, shook his head. "We don't know that she did. And even if she did, there's no way they'd even think of harming her. They're agents for crying out loud." Okay, so maybe my hypothesis was stupid, but I was desperate for an answer, not to mention, this wouldn't be the first time agents had turned rogue. Look at Piranha and her crew. If that had taught me anything, it taught me that you can't trust someone just because they hold a certain job. Now wasn't the time or place to remind Will of that, so I let it slide. We needed to figure out the why and who; then we'd be more likely to figure out the where.

"She hasn't gone to ground again, has she?" Imani's question was totally valid. Angelica still hadn't explained where she'd been when she'd been in hiding before we took RP down. We figured it had something to do with the PIB directors and Chad, but she wasn't talking.

We crossed a bridge over a canal. "Mum, do you think she has?" If anyone knew, she would. Since she'd been living with us, they'd spent a lot of time together, and because my mother was the closest friend Angelica had, chances were, she'd confided in her. Not that Angelica would definitely have confided in anyone, but on the small chance she had, my mother would be it.

"No, definitely not." Just over the bridge, she turned right. "This is it." We stood at one of the entries to a large square. Four-storey homes and a smattering of buildings with ground-floor shops ringed the open area. Mum walked to the middle of it, the sun shining brightly. A group of pigeons took brief flight at my mother's approach but landed nearby. "They found her here."

Will folded his arms as he looked at the now-empty spot. He slowly turned three hundred and sixty degrees, surveying our surroundings as he did so. "Well, that's an obvious place. Whoever did this didn't want it to go unnoticed."

Imani nodded, then looked at my mother. "Did they record any magic signatures?"

Mum's brow furrowed. "There weren't any. Looks like she was made into a sculpture somewhere else and transferred via a doorway. Locals said she was there for a few hours before anyone thought to tell the police. It was only when a witch neighbour friend of hers saw her and realised the sculpture was eerily similar. She called the PIB rather than the police."

"Do we know her name?" Will asked.

Mum answered, "Violetta Brambilla."

Will made a bubble of silence and looked at me. "Lily, can you do your thing?"

"Yes." Mum knew about my talent, but she'd never seen it in action—we'd shown her the photos of her being hunted. Her reaction had been part shock and part pride. Once she'd got over that, anger slid in, and she thanked me for killing Dana's father. Thank God we'd given her closure and those maniacs didn't get away.

I walked about twelve feet away so I had a better visual of the whole area. I took the lens cap off, flicked on the Nikon, and lifted it to my face. "Show me Angelica leaving this spot last night." There she was, walking towards me, poker face intact, one hand in her pocket. I snapped a shot and showed it to everyone. "She doesn't look particularly stressed." I took my camera back. Something was bugging me. Angelica rarely put her hand in her pocket, which might seem like nothing, but had she found something that she didn't hand over to the PIB? And if not, why? I lifted my camera again and stepped closer to where the sculpture would have been. "Show me Angelica finding something last night."

The light waned, and pretty Venetian lamps lit the square. Angelica was crouching at the foot of the glass sculpture of a woman who was about five foot four and rather wide. I snapped a shot and moved closer, until I was right next to her. I crouched and focussed on what Angelica was picking up. Thankfully, the PIB had set up a floodlight on the statue, and visibility was excellent. Pinched between Angelica's thumb and pointer finger was a pearlescent blue button. *Click.*

I stood and showed Will, Imani, and Mum. "She found something."

Imani pressed her lips together for a while, likely thinking. "How would the killer know she'd found evidence? I mean, why target her and not any of the other agents if they didn't know?"

Will scratched his head. "Opportunity? The other agents didn't return to a hotel late at night. They would've gone somewhere private, made a doorway, and left. Maybe all they're trying to do is distract us from figuring anything out by making more work for us?"

That didn't make total sense. "But it's not for *us*. No one knows you guys are all agents, do they?"

Mum shrugged. "We haven't been making a big deal out of it, but we were all in that courtyard after Mr Dal Lago was discovered."

"Which might mean that the killer works at the hotel," said Imani. "It's looking more and more like the wife, wouldn't you say?"

"Or a jealous lover." I wasn't letting them forget that.

Will put his hands on his hips. "Right, so we still have as many suspects as before, but we have a potential motive for why Angelica was targeted." He looked at me. "Can you take some pictures of everyone who was at the scene when Angelica picked up that button?"

"Can do." I lifted my camera again and asked the question. This one was tricker, because the square was large. I panned around. The two Italian PIB agents who'd originally come to the hotel were there, as were two other men dressed in PIB get-up—black suit and tie with white shirt. A couple of lights were on in the windows surrounding the square. A group of eleven young men and women stood in one corner of the square smoking, and a dark figure watched from a shadowed doorway. I shuddered before walking up to the doorway. I frowned. There was no light there as it was at the far side of the square. The person was shorter and slimmer than me, but they had a large hat pulled over their head and a long coat on, which was super unusual considering how warm it was. Hands in pockets, posture hunched, I couldn't tell if it was a man or woman. Likely they were taller than they appeared too. *Click. Click.* Was it Mrs Dal Lago? It was probably too small to be Lorenzo—he was a few inches taller than me and had a bigger build. But then again, what if Lorenzo and Mrs Dal Lago were working together? I had no idea why they would be, but considering all options was sensible at this stage.

As soon as I made it back to our group, I handed the camera to Will. They all looked at the pictures. Will zoomed in on where the face should be, but the gloom fuzzed out any details. "Right. That's probably our guy… or girl."

Imani sighed. "But it doesn't really help anything."

Mum cocked her head to the side. "Well, it's better than nothing. We have an approximate height and build."

At least we had something to work with now. "So he or she

has likely followed Angelica back to the hotel and kidnapped her on the way?"

Imani nodded. "Looks like it."

"Agreed," said Will. "Let's follow Angelica back to the hotel and see what happened."

"Sounds good." I lifted the camera and pointed it back the way we'd come—the way Angelica should've been heading if she'd decided to return to the hotel. "Show me Angelica after she left here last night." There she was, her back to me. "She went this way. We'll follow her until we can't see her anymore."

I kept my distance to see if the person had come after her. Once we left the square and turned a couple of corners, I stopped. "Angelica went this way, but that person in the coat didn't follow."

Imani looked at me. "If they were from the hotel, maybe they knew she was heading back there, but they had another way to get there?"

"Could be," said Will. "Let's keep following Angelica and see what happened."

Every few steps I asked my magic to show me Angelica on her way back to the hotel. It was tedious but effective. The going was slow, but we finally made it to within fifteen feet of the hotel before she disappeared. I lowered the camera and lifted it again. "Show me the second before Angelica disappeared." There she was, in the last place my camera had shown me. I wrinkled my brow. "She made it to here. And she didn't turn around and leave either. She must've gone through a portal. And no one else was in sight." I'd double-checked all the doorways too.

I showed everyone the photos. "Actually, let me get a picture of her from the front." I'd been photographing her from behind the whole way. Had she still been relaxed at the moment before she disappeared? "Show me Angelica the hundredth of a second before she disappeared last night." She materialised in my view, and I walked around to see her from the front. It was dark, but there were sconce lights on the outside of the hotel and some moonlight—enough to see her expression. I scrunched my forehead. "Correct me if I'm wrong, but does she look… puzzled to you?"

I handed my camera to Will, whose brow furrowed as soon as he saw the pic. Imani and Mum looked at the screen with him. Mum rubbed her chin. "She's definitely wondering about something. Look at the tension in her body. She's preparing for something."

Imani nodded. "You're right. Maybe she sensed magic? Did someone cast a spell on her?"

Will handed my camera back, and I lifted it to my face. "Show me someone casting a spell on Angelica." Nothing happened. "Maybe whoever it was magicked themselves back to the hotel reception room or another nearby building and was watching from a window?"

Will did his own glancing around, then shook his head. "There's no way we'll see anyone in a dark window at night." He took my camera off me and zoomed in on some windows in the background of the last photo I'd taken. "You could take closer photos of the windows, just in case. You'd only need to take the ones around the hotel. Unless it was a ridiculously powerful witch, there's no way they could cast a doorway around her from too far away."

"Plus whatever other spell they needed." My mum rubbed her chin. "They would've had to knock her out just before throwing the doorway around her or when she reached wherever they took her. There's no way they'd be able to overpower her otherwise, and she would've returned by now."

Will's deep voice held a note of worry. "You're right."

I grabbed my camera back and pointed it at different buildings, each time asking my magic to show me if there was someone in any of the windows. Nothing. Nausea swirled in my stomach. This was looking worse by the minute. "So, now what?"

Will held up his phone. I'll call Agent Tondato and start the process. We need to go through all the evidence so far as a group. We'll grab Beren and Liv and organise a meeting with our Italian counterparts. Then we'll comb the hotel for any more evidence, see if they missed something the first time." Despite feeling ill, my stomach grumbled. Will stared at me. "Have you had breakfast?"

"No. Have you?"

"No. So, maybe we have a quick bite first because we have a long day ahead. Come on." He led the way to the hotel restaurant where breakfast was still being served. After calling Beren to get him and Liv to meet us there, he called Agent Tondato and set up a meeting at their office in Trieste in an hour.

Breakfast was a delicious, if silent, affair. I managed to down two cappuccinos and a pastry that had chocolate inside. Unless we found Angelica, this food would be the highlight of my day. The nausea returned when I contemplated not finding her. Crap. The longer she was gone, the less likely we'd find her alive—isn't that what they said on cop shows? Gah. We'd just have to find her today, then. We hadn't survived the most dangerous group of evil people for her to die while we were supposed to be relaxing on holiday nowhere near anyone who had it in for us. I sighed.

Mum, who was sitting next to me, placed her arm around me. "Angelica's a survivor. We'll find her alive."

I gave Mum a sad smile. "I'm an optimist, but you always out-positivitied me. I hope you're right."

"So do I, sweetie. So do I."

CHAPTER 6

"Please, sit." Agent Tondato indicated the chairs around a light-coloured timber conference table that wasn't quite as big as the one at headquarters. Black leather chairs with polished steel frames surrounded the table, and I sat next to Will. Beren sat opposite us next to Agent Tondato's offsider, Agent Matteo Rinaldi, who wore his dark hair short. He was an average-height, wiry man, likely in his forties, with a five o'clock shadow. Agent Tondato sat at the head of the table. "Would you like a coffee?"

"No thanks." Will leaned forward and placed his arms on the table. "We'd like to get straight to it, if that's okay?

Agent Tondato gave a nod. "Of course. Agent DuPree is missing, and you want to find her quickly, no?"

Will's jaw flexed, his frustration showing. "Yes. The longer this takes, the worse the likely outcome. Now, can you tell us where you're up to with this case. We're assuming her disappearance is linked to her involvement in the Dal Lago case."

The Italian agent nodded again. "And you've checked with your head office?"

Will shut his eyes, then opened them. "Yes, of course. We're supposed to be here on holiday, and Angelica would never just leave for an extended period without telling someone. If you could please take us through the case so far, we would very much appreciate it."

Grrrr. I was ready to stomp over there and slap the information out of that Italian guy. Why was he being so difficult? Maybe he was just an annoying person.

"Okay. We will help you. But this is highly unusual. We don't normally share information, and this is not the only case we are working on, so we cannot move as fast as you are asking." Magic tickled my scalp—I was assuming Agent Tondato's—and a large file appeared on the table in front of Will. "All the information you need is there, but it's in Italian." Wow, he was being super helpful… not.

Will stared at the guy. He opened his mouth to say something, then closed it again. He breathed out of his nose loudly. "It's actually fine. I know a translation spell." Will's magic caressed my scalp. Nothing appeared to have changed, but when he opened the file and spread out some papers so we could take a look at them, the text was in English. Nice work.

As we all read through the notes, Agent Tondato gave us an overview. "Our main suspect is still Lorenzo Zanini, even though he has an alibi. It wouldn't be the first time that family lied or that evidence was tampered with."

Will had perused most of the documents. "Why isn't the victim's wife listed as a suspect? They were having money problems and arguing. Shouldn't we at least ask her for her magic signature?"

Agent Tondato pursed his lips. "Your Agent DuPree asked

me that question, and I told her that we are a passionate people."

I rolled my eyes. "And 'it's not enough of a reason.' Yes, we know. It is enough of a reason where we come from, and considering that Angelica disappeared close to our hotel, maybe Mrs Dal Lago had something to do with it."

Beren gave me a subtle head shake from across the table, his green eyes imploring me to be quiet. Oops. Dammit. Me and my big mouth.

Agent Tondato rubbed his forehead. "And how do you know this, Miss…?"

"Bianchi. Lily Bianchi."

"Oh, you have an Italian background, *sì?*"

"Yes. My father, but he's dead." I frowned. Maybe he'd give me sympathy and agree to get a warrant for this woman's magic signature.

"Okay, Miss Bianchi. How do you know she went missing near your 'otel?"

I swallowed. Now what was I supposed to say? "Ah… my mother and Angelica share a… connection. After my mother went missing for ten years and we got her back again, we spelled them so they could sense each other if they were within half a mile of each other. They're best friends, you know. Mum remembers waking up maybe an hour or so after Angelica left to see you. She sensed Angelica was near, but then she lost the… ah… feeling after a moment and thought she must have imagined it because she was half asleep." Beren blinked and pressed his lips together. I gave Agent Tondato a toothy grin, and Will erected his poker face. *Please buy my crap. Please buy my crap.*

Agent Tondato stared at me, then regarded Will and

Beren. Finally, he said, "Okay, then. Maybe we can confirm this with some security footage, no?"

Will cleared his throat. "Yes, that would be a good idea. Can you do that this morning?"

"Sí. Once we confirm she was there that night, we can… make… more investigation at the 'otel."

Will nodded. "Thank you. Also, I'd like a favour, please."

"Sí?"

"My sister is also an agent—Sarah Blakesley. She'll be here later this afternoon. I would like her to sit in on any interviews you do. She's fluent in Italian. I'd like to sit in, too, to observe, if you don't mind." Will couldn't speak fluent Italian, but maybe he could read body language. I was pretty sure they studied that at agent school—reading body language was a useful skill in solving crimes and dealing with people who were likely to lie. If only James was here, we could use his skills. Although, could he pick up if someone was lying in another language that he couldn't understand? Hmm, I wasn't sure how his talent worked. Why was nothing ever straightforward?

The balding head agent of this PIB office folded his arms and observed Will for a moment. He then shared a look with his fellow agent, who'd kept quiet the whole time. There'd be no reason to say no… well, except if they were hiding something.

Finally, Agent Tondato spoke. "Okay. This is fine. I have your number, and I will message you when we are coming to question Signora Dal Lago. It won't be till later because we have to visit Rome for another investigation." Sounded like there was plenty of crime happening over here. Kind of like in the UK. It never ended.

Still, they were being helpful enough, and the tension in my shoulders loosened. Now hopefully we'd get somewhere.

My gaze caught a photo of the female victim, the one Angelica had gone to see before she went missing. I picked it up and read the text underneath. Violetta Brambilla. Eighty-four-year-old witch, and a widow. "Do you know why she was killed?"

"No," Agent Tondato said. "But we have our... how you say... theories. She maybe saw something, or she knew the alibi for Lorenzo was false. We're following it up today."

That was super weird. "Interesting, isn't it? You'd think if you wanted to kill someone that old, you'd do it subtly. If you made it look like a heart attack, no one would even bother checking—they'd just take it for granted. Why would the killer draw attention to themselves like that?" We'd briefly touched on this in the square, but I wanted to see if the Italians had any ideas.

Will looked at Agent Tondato. "So, the killer was making a point. But why?"

Agent Tondato's offsider spoke. "It's simple. Arrogance or a warning. If anyone else knows something, they won't talk."

Agent Tondato's magic vibrated my scalp, and all the papers and file disappeared. He stood. "We will gather the security footage. I will call you back here to watch them when it is done. Maybe in one or two hours?"

Will stood. "Okay. Grazie." I smiled at Will's one Italian word. Even I knew how to say thank you. But something was better than nothing. Will held his hand out, and they shook. Beren and I stood. Agent Tondato shook Beren's hand but didn't bother to reach out for mine. Well, stuff you, then, Mr Sexist Pig.

At least I knew the landing address for the hotel's reception room. I didn't bother saying goodbye to the Italian agents. Instead, I turned to Will. "I'll see you back at the hotel." I made my doorway and stepped through. Why did some men have to be so rude? That guy didn't know it, but I could outmagic him any day.

I buzzed the intercom. After a minute or so, Isabella, the old lady, answered the door. Her weak smile didn't reach her blue eyes. "Ciao." The stress of having her boss killed was probably getting to her and everyone else who worked at the hotel.

"Ciao." I smiled. "Grazie." I hurried past her and up the stairs to my room. I went to the bathroom, then texted my mother to see where she, Liv, and Imani were. A text came back straight away. *We're in my room.* That made sense. Just in case a miracle occurred and Angelica found her way out of her predicament, she'd go back to her room, likely thinking one of us would be there waiting for her.

I texted Will to tell him where we all were, then rushed to my mother's room and knocked. "It's me, Mum."

She opened the door. Her gaze searched mine, worry wrinkling her brow. "Any news?"

"Not really." I went in and shut the door. Imani and Liv sat at the two-seater table, and my mum plonked herself on her bed. I sat at the end of Angelica's bed and made a bubble of silence. "The Italian agents are going to pull security footage for us. They said they should be ready to view in about an hour. Once they confirm she disappeared—because I couldn't exactly show them my photos or tell them why—they've agreed to question the wife."

Imani turned her phone over and over in her hands. "Well, that's a start."

"They've also agreed to let Sarah and Will sit in on the interview."

"That's something, at least," my mother said. "Do they have any suspects other than the wife and Lorenzo?"

"No. I don't know. These guys are pretty hopeless, or they're secretive. I'm not sure which. How did they ever get to represent the PIB?"

Liv raised a brow. "You're serious, right? I give you one word: Chad."

I sighed. "You make a very good point. There are probably lots of Chads heading up PIB departments all over the place. I should think before I speak."

Imani smirked. "Yes, you should."

My mother shook her head, and her shoulders sagged. "It's not like the old days. Most agents were competent and professional. We weren't underfunded back then. It's sad to see the bureau in such a state. I dread to think what's going to happen in the future. Without a strong bureau, bad witches are going to create havoc, and there won't be anyone there to hold them accountable."

A vibration snaked down my spine. "That sounds scary. I hope they fix it before it's too late." I hoped that creepy sensation wasn't a premonition of worse things to come. Now that RP was all but destroyed, things should improve, shouldn't they?

A knock sounded on the door, and I jumped. Mum looked at me and chuckled as she stood. "For a brave woman, you sure are nervous. I'm still surprised you didn't grow out of it."

"I blame you and Dad. It's in my genes. I can't help it if I got some dud ones. You should've done a better job."

Mum opened the door. "Come in." She returned to her spot on the bed, and Will came and sat next to me. Beren gave Liv a quick kiss on the lips and sat on the end of Mum's bed.

"Well, this is cosy, loves." Imani shut the door, turned her gaze on Will, and cast another bubble of silence. "I'm assuming that interviewing Mr Dal Lago's wife might uncover some other suspects we've missed?"

"We can hope. As well as that, I want Lily to observe Mrs Dal Lago's magical strength. If she did do it, maybe she had help." Will looked at me. "Is that okay?"

I shrugged. "I'm happy to do that, but how am I supposed to find out? I can't exactly shadow her all day. I don't know what her magic feels like, so it's not as if I can sit somewhere on-site and just wait."

Liv's eyes lit up. "We can orchestrate something. Maybe you could make a mess in front of her and get her to clean it up."

I blinked. "That would be rude of me, not cleaning up after myself, since I'm a witch."

Liv smiled. "So? Who cares? Be rude. If that's what it takes to get some info that might help, do it. Does it matter what she thinks of you?"

"Hmm, I suppose not." I turned and looked at Will. "But couldn't I just be there during the interview when they ask for her magic signature? They'd have to make her cast a small spell to get it, right?"

"Yes, but they'll cast a magic-dampening spell to make sure she doesn't draw too much power—no one wants a suspect to go berserk and escape. That's likely to affect your perception of it." Will grabbed my hand and squeezed it gently, sincerity leaching from his gaze. "Don't worry. I'm sure you'll have no trouble making a mess in front of her."

My mother laughed, and Liv snorted. I narrowed my eyes. "Very funny." I twisted around and glared at my mother. "I thought you were supposed to be on my side?"

"I am on your side, but I'm also honest. You were always

so messy. The number of times your father and I grounded you for not tidying your room…. And don't get me started on what a grubby eater you were. I had to have a mat under your chair until you were twelve, and even then, you didn't need to be a genius to work out where you'd sat."

"Why did you hide that you were a witch back then? You could've just magicked it away instead of used the vacuum cleaner." My mother licked her lips. This was a subject I hadn't broached with her yet, and I was pretty sure now wasn't the time, but my brain was slow to catch up. "Don't worry, Mum. We don't have to do this now. But be warned that I want the answer to that question when this is all over and done with. When my twenty-fourth birthday came around, it was one hell of a bad week." Not only had my electronics gone haywire the day after my birthday—my phone didn't work properly, my coffee machine died—but that was also the day I found out James was missing. I could safely say that it had been the worst birthday ever, and thanks to not knowing my mother was a witch, I'd had no warning.

"I'm sorry, sweetie. I had my reasons, and I'll be happy to share them with you later… when we have Angelica safe and sound."

"Okay." I wasn't going to give her a hard time. None of us were in the mood, and Mum had been through enough. I didn't miss the sympathetic look Liv gave me, though. It was nice that she cared.

Will looked at his phone. "Agent Tondato should be contacting me in about forty-five minutes to an hour, so let's get Lily downstairs and fishing for some info. Mrs Dal Lago might go into hiding once they've spoken to her, so now's our best chance."

"Can I go with her?" asked Liv.

"Me too, please." Imani smirked.

I squinted at both of them. "What gives?"

Imani answered, "We want to see you make a mess. It should be fun."

My top lip hitched up at the corner. "Weirdos. Out of all the things you could be doing in Venice, that's your choice?"

Liv nodded. "Yep." She looked at Will. "So can we?"

He chuckled. "I guess so. But don't look suspicious."

Imani gave him a "you have got to be kidding me look," then deadpanned, "I'm a professional."

I jumped up. "Okay, then. Let's get this over and done with. I reckon we head to the bar and order a milky cocktail. That should spill nicely everywhere, and it'll stink if she doesn't clean it up straight away."

My friends stood, and we made our way to the door. "Ooh, I know!" Liv was a little too excited, so I was dreading what she was going to say. "Can you vomit at will? No one could ignore that."

I looked at her as if she was one sandwich short of a picnic. "Ah, no. What the hell, woman? Maybe *you* could do it since you think it's such a great idea?"

Her excitement disappeared. "No, no, it's okay. I don't know how to do that. The cocktail idea is fine."

I rolled my eyes and opened the door. "Come on." The trick was going to be finding Mrs Dal Lago. If she wasn't around, we'd miss our chance. We reached the bottom of the stairs. We were in luck; she was manning—or was that womanning?—the small reception desk. I smiled. "Hi."

Her return smile was subdued. "Hello. Are you enjoying your stay?"

Liv answered, "Yes, thanks. Venice is so beautiful, and your hotel is full of charm. How long have you had it?"

"Many years. This is our seventeenth year." She frowned and looked down at her hands on the shelf on the inside of the reception desk. When she looked up again, her jaw bunched, as if she were holding something in. "Now I must run it without my husband. It will be difficult."

"I'm so sorry." Imani's voice was gentle. "We're sorry for your loss."

Mrs Dal Lago gave us a sad smile. "Thank you. Now, if you'll excuse me, I must get back to work."

We said goodbye and strolled down the hall to the bar where we ordered our drinks, and I paid. We moved away from the bar and stood in the middle of the room. I made a bubble of silence. "So, she seemed genuinely sad, didn't she."

Imani nodded. "Yes. Although you'd think she'd be happy to be rid of him so she could enjoy her dalliances without his disapproval."

She was forgetting something. "But they had an open marriage." I sniffed my chocolatey cocktail. It smelled so sweet and yummy. I needed enough to make a mess, but surely I was entitled to a taste? I sucked a small amount through the straw. Oh my God, so good. It was going to be such a shame to spill it on the floor.

Liv sipped her red wine. "I don't know about that. I mean, maybe they did, but what if he didn't want one? What if he agreed so he wouldn't lose her? Have we found anyone he was having an affair with?"

I shrugged. "I have no idea. I'll have to ask Will to bring it up with Mr Sexist Agent."

Imani's brow furrowed. "What?"

"When we left their office before, Agent Tondato shook everyone's hands except mine... because I was the woman."

Liv pressed her lips together. "How do you know it was

because of that? Maybe he knows you're not an agent, and that's why?"

"I s'pose you could be right, but either way, he doesn't respect me."

Imani slapped my back. "Don't worry about it. We respect you. Will, Beren, Angelica, and your mum respect you. Even the squirrels respect you. We're the only ones who matter."

"Thanks. Now I'd better keep that respect. It's time to find out how strong this witch is." I wished we could find out right now if she'd taken Angelica. Not knowing where she was and how she was, killed me.

As we got to the doorway, the bartender called out. "Excuse me! You can't take your drinks out there."

"Keep going," I whispered. "Pretend we didn't hear." I wasn't stopping for anything.

"Hey!" I didn't dare look behind, but he was probably on his way to drag us back inside.

I jogged down the hallway towards the reception desk. Thank God Mrs Dal Lago was still there. I hadn't figured out how I was going to spill it—maybe pretend to trip?—but I needn't have worried. Imani grabbed my arm, the one holding the cocktail. "Wait! We can't leave the bar with these drinks, Lily." She jerked me to a stop. It would've been enough to spill some but not all of my drink, so I let go of my glass, feigning surprise.

"Oh no! Look what you did!" I put my hands on my hips. "You'll have to buy me another one. That was really good, and it was expensive."

The bartender had caught up to us, and Mrs Dal Lago had come out from behind the reception desk. What if she made the bartender clean it up? I turned to him. "Sorry, but I needed to go to the toilet, and it's not safe to leave a drink unattended. Do you think you could make me another? This lady will pay for it." I pointed at Imani.

"Mio Dio." Mrs Dal Lago said something else in Italian, her tone of voice… passionate. She waved one arm in the air and shook her head. Before she had time to ask him to clean it up, I took his hand and dragged him down the hallway.

"Come on. I really need another drink. Maybe you could make it while I'm in the loo, and when I get back, I promise I'll stay in here to drink it."

He tugged his arm out of my grip. "You are crazy, lady. I'll make you a drink, but don't grab me again."

I put my hands up. "Sorry. I'm just really thirsty."

Familiar magic tingled my scalp—I remembered it from the morning Mrs and Mr Dal Lago had fought. I turned. Mrs Dal Lago was casting a spell to clean up my mess. Her aura shone brightly as she did it, amplified by her magic use. But it wasn't out-of-the-ordinary bright. Her power was average, and I doubted enough to cast a travel spell from a long way away. I wasn't sure how much magic it took to turn someone into glass, but surely it was more than average?

I gave Imani a nod. She smiled at Mrs Dal Lago. "I'm so sorry about my friend. We can't take her anywhere." She rolled her eyes as if I were such a troublemaker.

Mrs Dal Lago looked at Imani but didn't smile. "Just make sure you stay in there or in your room with the drinks, or we could lose our licence."

Imani nodded. "Of course. Sorry. We'll just go back in the bar and make sure we do that." Imani and Liv sat on one of the couches in the corner furthest from the bar.

I went to the bathroom because the ruse needed to be believable. When I returned, I paid for my new drink and went and sat with Liv and Imani. I waved my cocktail at Imani. "You owe me ten euros for this."

Her mouth dropped open. "You cheapskate. Are you kidding, love? You're the one who dropped it."

"You grabbed me." I created a bubble of silence. "I'm just kidding. I wanted to make sure they bought the charade. And I was supposed to make a mess. Remember?"

Her eyes widened. "You had me, love. I thought you were serious."

Liv had an "I'm impressed" expression. "You fooled me too. Nice acting."

"Thanks. Maybe I should consider a career change." I slid my phone from my pocket. "I'll message Will and let him know… about Mrs D's magic, not my potential career change."

Imani chuckled and shook her head. "What did you find out?"

"Her magic feels normal and boring with a hint of flirtation. And don't ask me how I know. It just is. Anyway, it's of average powerfulness. Nothing special. She's definitely a fair bit weaker than all of us. It'd be a struggle for her to cast a spell from far away, and even if she managed it, the vibration would have woken all of us. But she is a similar size and build to that person in my photo with the coat on."

Since we'd rescued my mother, I'd been reading up on magic and the level of power needed for different spells. Part of it was to try and find a way to heal Mum, so she could use her magic again, and the other was to understand exactly how powerful I was. I'd managed to kill Piranha, even though she had a return to sender up. My spell had destroyed hers. I didn't know exactly how powerful I was, but it was humbling to know I had more power than probably 95 per cent of witches, at least based on my power point score, which was kind of like an IQ test but for magic. My skill level wasn't as high as some witches with less power—I definitely needed more practice, especially with complex spells—but I had potential. The fact that I could gauge how powerful another witch was and detect how their magic felt was a testament to my innate ability. We'd all decided to keep this as secret as possible—story of my adult life. The less magic I performed in front of other witches, the better. If another witch could feel power levels as I could—and there were a few—I might become a target… yet again. Seemed like as free as I finally was, I would always have to watch my back.

Imani stared at the far wall for a moment. "Right, so she's probably not our suspect, but we can't rule her out just yet. If it's not her, and it's not the glass-blower guy, then who? What are we missing?"

I turned my head and checked out the bartender. Was he jealous of his lover's husband? He'd made our drinks with magic, but it didn't feel particularly special either, so I discounted him. Was Mr Dal Lago a bad boss? Or did he owe more people money?

Will, Beren, and my mother walked in. Beren went straight to the bar, and Will and Mum came and sat on the couch opposite where Liv, Imani, and I sat. Mum smiled. "Glad to see whatever mess you made didn't get you banned from the hotel. What's the verdict?"

I made a bubble of silence, and my eyes widened. "You thought I might get banned?"

She shrugged. "You never know."

My own mother had sent me to the potential slaughter. Okay, so I might have been overdramatising it, but still…. "I can't believe you let me do it while thinking that."

"Don't be such a drama queen, Lily. You and Will could've gone and stayed somewhere else. But this was important, and I couldn't think of another way for you to figure it out."

"Speaking of which," Will chimed in. "What's the verdict?"

"I don't think it's her. Average power at best. Definitely not enough to cast a travel spell from afar. And whatever spell they knocked Angelica out with—assuming that's how she didn't manage to escape—there's no way she could've managed that simultaneously from that distance."

Will rubbed the back of his neck. "She might just be an accomplice. At least that's another piece of the puzzle. We'll know more once we interview her."

Beren arrived at the table with drinks for Will, Mum, and himself. He sat and cast another bubble of silence. "So, spill." I let Will fill him in as I finished my cocktail.

Even though we'd just learned something, we weren't figuring this out fast enough. Was Angelica okay? Was she even still alive? She had to be. At least a glass sculpture of her hadn't turned up yet, and since the killer had done that to two people already, I assumed he or she would likely do that to Angelica too. I pulled my phone out of my pocket and tried her number. It went straight to voicemail. Damn. Frustration and fear built inside me. My leg bounced up and down. "We have to do something."

Will's gaze jumped to me. "We are doing something."

"It's not enough. We need to move faster." How could I make them see?

Imani rubbed my back. "We're doing everything we can right now. We don't have jurisdiction here, and we can't contact Chad—that would be the last thing Angelica would want. Imagine how insufferable he'd be? He'll either make it harder for us to find her, or he'll lord it over her once she's found."

"But what if she's... dead?" It took all my effort to slow my breaths. Was I almost having a panic attack?

Will looked at me, care and love shining from his eyes. His voice was softer than normal. "If she's already dead, Lily, it will make no difference how long we take. But I don't think she's dead."

I couldn't believe she was dead either... at least, I was trying to reserve judgement for my own sanity. "You don't think? But you don't know." He wasn't going to banish my worry that easily. Yes, worrying when you couldn't do anything about it wasn't productive, but it was human, and I was so very human.

"No, I don't know, but I can't entertain anything else. Angelica's resourceful. She always has a return to sender up. Whatever they've done couldn't be too bad."

Liv frowned. "If she always has a return to sender up, how could they render her unconscious... assuming that's what happened?"

"A tranquilliser gun?" Beren suggested. "Maybe after they got her through the doorway? One of them could've made the portal, and if someone else was waiting on the other side...."

I sucked in a breath. "Oh, well, that's just such an improvement. Jeez Louise. Way to make me feel better."

Imani ignored my outburst. "You could be right, B. Maybe when she reached the destination, they hit her over the head? We could be looking at more than one suspect."

"Agreed," said Beren. He looked at his phone. "Hopefully Agent Tondato is going to call soon."

I jumped up. "I can't sit here and just wait. I'm going for a walk. I'll be back in thirty. Text me if anything happens before then."

Imani and Will looked at each other. Imani stood. "I'm not needed right now either. I'll join you." She smiled and slid her arm around mine.

I looked at our linked arms. "Afraid I'll run away or do something crazy?"

"Yes. More so the second option rather than the first. If Angelica's been targeted because of this investigation, we're all potential targets."

Will looked around at our group. "Imani's right. None of us have found anything yet, but who knows what the killer's thinking? From now on, none of us goes anywhere by ourselves if we can help it. Have someone else with you at all times." His gaze pinged from my mother to Liv. "And you two, don't be with just each other. I think it's prudent for you to have a witch with you at all times."

My mother swallowed, her shoulders drooping. This must be so hard for her. She was once almost as powerful as me, or just as powerful. Now she had nothing but a useless trickle. At least she still had her fighting skills. She'd started weights as well. Even though she wasn't back to 100 per cent healthy, she was looking way better than the day we rescued her. She'd been pale, skinny, haunted. Since then, she'd regained some colour and weight, and the light in her eyes, whilst not as vibrant as I'd like, was slowly brightening. "That's a good plan, William." She stood. "I'm going to accompany Lily and Imani." She made her way to me and smiled. "I'm not cramping your style, am I?"

I chuckled. "Never." I linked my arm through hers.

"I'll stay with B for now, if that's okay. If he needs to leave, I'll give you a call, Lil. Is that okay?"

I smiled at Liv. "Of course. We won't go far. I want to be close in case anyone needs us after the interview. I feel like I haven't explored this hotel enough. Can we go and feed the pigeons in the courtyard?"

"Why would you want to do that?" Will asked, his tone of voice suggesting he thought my motive wasn't feeding the pigeons. He'd be right.

"Just because." I gave him an innocent smile. "Toodle-pip." Before he could ask any more questions, I turned and made my way to the door, dragging Mum and Imani with me since our arms were interlinked. Once we were striding down the hallway, we dropped arms, and Imani gave me a "what are you up to?" look. "You'll see."

Once in the courtyard, I pulled out my phone and looked at Imani and Mum. "I'd love to take a photo of you both. We've hardly taken any of us since we got here. Can you stand in the corner over there, next to the olive tree?" There was a small tree in a terracotta pot, and if I stayed where I was, the spot where they found the statue the other night was in between me and them. I only needed my talent, so it was unlikely anyone would even know I was using my power. But I had to find more clues. Angelica's life could depend on it. *Don't think about whether she's still alive.* I pushed my worrying thoughts away and held up my phone now that Imani and Mum were standing on either side of the tree. Being the smart ladies they were, they hadn't asked any questions.

I brought up the photo app and held up my phone. *Show me the person casting the spell on Mr Dal Lago the other night.* Day morphed to night, the courtyard faintly illuminated. But no one was here. Damn. I took the shot just because. He must've been magicked here after the deed was done. I cut off my magic. "Smile." Mum and Imani smiled, and I took another pic. "I'm done. Thanks."

"Can I see?" Imani asked as she came over. I showed her both photos.

Her face fell. "Oh. I see."

"At least we know something else now."

"Indeed, we do," said my mother.

"I don't know why *we* didn't do this before." Imani feigned cluelessness.

"Because *someone* asked me not to." I glared at my mum, hoping she knew I meant Angelica and not her. It was hard having a secret conversation out in the open. We could've used a bubble of silence, but it would look too suss. It had been easier in the bar with background music and leaving a decent distance between us and the bartender. Out here, the noise bounced off the walls and paving. If we were trying to catch someone who worked here, the less suspicion we aroused, the better.

"You know me, sweetie. I hate having my photo taken." Phew, she got it. Of course she did. She was an agent and my mother. It was unlikely that anything would slip past her. "What do you want to do now?"

We needed to have a chat somewhere we could make a BOS. I had a genius idea to run by them… okay, so I thought it was genius. General consensus had yet to be determined. "I could be talked into window shopping for a while."

Mum smiled. "Great. Let's go."

We crossed the square and slipped into an alleyway where we had plenty of shops to choose from. I picked the first shop that had glass figurines in the window and stopped, then made a BOS. "So, he was turned to glass somewhere else and moved. But it likely wouldn't have been from that far away, considering how much power they would've used to put him into that state."

Imani looked in the window. "I agree. What's your plan?"

"Retrace his steps on the day he went missing. Well, as best I can. Obviously, if he made a doorway at some stage, I can't follow that, but if he was turned to glass somewhere in the hotel…."

My mum nodded. "Good idea, sweetie. Although, instead of following him around, maybe you could just go into each room and ask if he was turned to glass in there?"

"That's going to be almost impossible. What if I get caught? I'm likely to end up in jail for trespassing, or whatever. I can't break into other guests' rooms. If I can follow him from a public area, it'll cut down the number of rooms I need to investigate."

Imani wrinkled her nose. "I doubt it was a guest… although we can't know for sure. In any case, I think it's best to start with rooms only staff are allowed in."

"I like that idea better. Less risks for me."

"We can keep a lookout too." Mum's suggestion had merit, although I didn't want her getting in the middle of it. The last thing she needed was to get arrested for aiding and abetting and ending up locked up after spending ten years confined by RP.

"I don't know." I blew out a breath. "The less you have to do with this, the better. I don't want you getting in trouble."

She stood taller, determination steeling her gaze. "I may have lost my magic, but I haven't lost all my skills. I can look after myself. Don't you worry about me." She used her "I'm the boss because I'm your mother" voice, and I wasn't going to argue with it. Old habits died hard… and so did cliches, apparently.

Imani slid her phone from her pocket. "I'm going to call Will, make sure he lets us know as soon as they're in the interview. At least Mrs Dal Lago won't be at the hotel then. That leaves the young man who took our bags, the bartender, kitchen staff, and that old lady, Isabella."

Unease slinked across my belly. "That's still a fair few witches. We'll just have to be careful. Do we know if the hotel staff sleep on-site?"

Imani shook her head. "No. Honestly, we know nothing at this point. Angelica was keeping us in the dark so she didn't ruin our holiday, but who knows how much the Italian agents know since they didn't want to blame the wife. It's like they don't want to do the work."

"They're more conservative than us when it comes to investigation techniques. I've come across it before. Just prior to falling pregnant with James, I was here for a month investigating a drug and arms ring. The London agents had to push for every bit of information to be gathered. It was hard work. The Italians like to take their time to the point of ridiculousness. It's just their way, I suppose. And you've been dealing with Agent Tondato, but I'll bet my second chance at life that he's got four or five levels of management above him that want to okay everything. Their bureaucracy is painful, but it is their way, and we're in their country, so...."

I sighed. "Well, I'm happy to risk being arrested if it means we can find Angelica. Worst comes to worst, I'll run, then come back to search. I won't give up till we find her."

Imani frowned. "Don't be silly."

Mum's brow wrinkled. "You were never patient, but don't lose the plot now, Lily. Please."

I sucked in a deep breath. "I'll try not to."

Imani dialled Will and put the phone to her ear. "Hey, it's

me. Just wondering when you're interviewing Mrs D." She listened for a minute. "Okay, excellent. I'll pass it on. Let me know when the interview is wrapping up. We're going to see if Lily can find anything at the hotel…. Yeah… okay. Bye."

I stared at her. "So? What's the latest?"

She smiled. "The security footage from both places they got it from showed her disappearing into thin air. They've confiscated it, too, since those places are run by non-witches. Had that footage reached the internet, we might have had some damage control to oversee."

I gave her a "you've got to be kidding" look. "Meh. No one believes that stuff. It's too easy to say it was doctored. I'm sure it would've been fine."

Imani raised a brow. "You're joking, right? I give you two words: flat-earthers. People believe all sorts of things on the internet."

She'd pointed out something so obvious that now I was embarrassed at being so stupid. Maybe I was only a few brain cells away from becoming a flat-earther. I needed to protect the brain matter I had left. "Hmm, okay. Fair enough. Point taken." Note to self: no more drinking, and buy a helmet. "So when is the interrogation taking place?"

Imani put her phone in the back pocket of her white shorts. "In fifteen minutes at the PIB Trieste office. Let's go back now, and we can start. You can take a photo of us in the hallway, get a pic of him last time he was there, see where he was headed. If we need to go into any restricted areas, we'll wait till Mrs D is gone, and I'd be happy to distract the bartender while Katerina acts as a lookout for you."

I nodded. "That's a great plan."

"Why, thank you, love."

"Mum?"

"Yes, sweetie."

"I'm going to cast a return to sender on you, just in case."

Her eyes widened. "You can't do that! It'll take too much power, especially if someone attacks me."

I smiled. "You do know I can handle it, right?"

Imani nodded slowly. "Some of the stuff your daughter's done in the last few months is ridiculous. She can totally handle it."

Mum's eyes shone with what might be pride, or maybe she had allergies and her eyes were watering? "I know. I'm sorry. I just…. I still see you as the innocent fourteen-year-old I waved goodbye to as the taxi drove your dad and me to the airport." She cupped my cheek with her hand. "I'm so sorry, Lily. If I'd known we weren't coming back and that we'd be leaving you and James as orphans…." She shook her head, and this time there were tears, one escaping to run down her cheek.

I pulled her into my arms and gave her a massive hug. "It's okay. You were fighting crime, trying to bring down the evilest witches on the planet. You couldn't have known what was coming. And James stepped up. He was the best big brother I could've wished for."

"But I can… well I used to be able to… tell the future, but I never saw it. I'm sorry, sweetie. I'm just so sorry." She shook as the tears well and truly took hold.

I rubbed her back. "It's okay, Mum. Why don't we talk about this later? We've got a job to do right now, and I know your agent instincts are still strong." I gave an extra squeeze. "I love you."

The crying stopped, and she sniffled. She stepped back and wiped her hand across her eyes and down her cheeks, then onto her knee-length green skirt. Lifting her head, she pinned me with a steadfast gaze. "Okay. I'm ready."

Church bells tolled, their melodic chimes falling around us and echoing throughout the laneway. If I closed my eyes, I could believe I was in the seventeenth century. The atmospheric ringing was something I'd miss when we left. Hopefully wherever Angelica was, she was alive and could hear those bells. A vibration of unease cascaded down my spine. I shuddered. Since I'd killed Dana and her dad, I'd managed to lead a peaceful few weeks. It was as if I wasn't ready for more danger. Did I have PTSD? Could witches get it? We probably could because we were still human. Nah, I didn't have it. Sure, I had nightmares sometimes and found it hard to fall asleep, but other than that, I'd been okay. I took a deep breath and shook it off. "Come on, then."

We began the short walk back to the hotel. By the time we reached the front door, my hands were sweating, and I was breathing way faster than what I should've been for a leisurely walk.

"Are you okay?" Imani gently held my chin and looked into my eyes.

"I'm, um…. I think I'm okay. Maybe I'm stressing because I don't want to put any of us in danger. I don't know." Or maybe I could tell that something bad was going to happen. *Argh, stop thinking, Lily!*

She released my chin and put a hand on my shoulder. "It's going to be okay, Lily. We need to save Angelica, and I'm pretty sure that nothing is going to happen right now. Maybe you should look into some counselling when we get home?"

"You're right. I know you are. Everything will be fine, as long as we find Angelica alive and well. And maybe I will see someone when I get home, but in the meantime, what do I do?"

"Adrenaline is part of the problem. You need to slow your

breathing. Just take deep, slow breaths. Okay?" Her magic tickled my scalp, and comforting warmth settled around me. How was she doing that? I'd have to ask her later.

She'd used her magic to help me feel better—the least I could do was do as she'd asked. "Okay." A pleasant memory blossomed in my head—the squirrels on the day we left to come here. I envisaged all my furry friends sitting around their miniature table, nibbling away. They were so cute! My heart stopped pounding, and the feeling of impending doom faded. I wiped my hands dry on my olive-green shorts. I could do this. Angelica needed me to do this. I nodded. "I'm ready."

Mum opened the door and held it for Imani and me. Mrs D wasn't at the front desk—the young man who'd taken our bags stood behind it, watching us come in. I gave him a wave. "Buongiorno." One of the only Italian non-food words I knew.

He gave a tentative smile. "Buongiorno." His smile disappeared, and he stared at the desktop. Bit of a shy fellow, apparently.

I stopped walking and addressed my companions. "We haven't taken any photos in the hotel yet! I want to remember this holiday forever. Plus, James will want to see the place. He could bring Mill here one day."

"Great idea." Mum smiled. "Where do you want us to stand?"

I shrugged. "Halfway between me and the bar. We can take photos in the bar later." I winked, and Mum and Imani laughed.

Imani tapped her nose with her index finger. "I'm onto you, lovie."

"What can I say? Those cocktails are to die for." Argh, why did I have to use that expression? I did not want to die for any reason, let alone for a cocktail. Way to remind myself about stressful stuff. I had a real knack for saying the wrong thing, even if I was just thinking to myself. Sheesh. *Please let Angelica be okay*.

Mum and Imani placed themselves further down the hallway and faced me, each with an arm around the back of the other. I lifted my phone and opened myself up to my internal magic and my talent. In my mind, I said, *Show me Mr Dal Lago the last time he was here. Where did he go straight from this hallway?* To Mum and Imani, I said, "Smile."

The lights dimmed in my screen, the hallway lit only by a couple of wall sconces. Mr Dal Lago's back was to me, at the far end of the hall, at the door next to the bar area entry—the office. His hand was on the doorknob, and he was by himself. I snapped a shot of him, then closed off my magic and snapped a pic of Mum and Imani—I might as well have some nice snaps too. "Lovely! Just what I wanted. Let's get a drink." We were spending so much time in the bar, the bartender probably thought we were alcoholics.

I ordered the drinks and took note of the bartender's magic as he created them in a jiffy. Hmm, he was a bit more powerful than Mrs D, but not by much. He likely wasn't our guy, unless he'd teamed up with her and they'd somehow managed it together. He magicked the drinks onto a tray and grinned. "Ciao, beautiful. Are you enjoying your stay?"

Oh, he was a charmer, even after telling me not to touch him earlier. Maybe he was desperate for a tip. Great. "Ah, yes, thank you. Venice is beautiful."

"Just like you." He leaned one elbow on the bar and waggled his eyebrows. "Want me to show you around later? I can show you all the pleasures of... Venice." Wow, what a proposition. How was I ever going to resist?

"Um, thank you, but no. I'm here with my fiancée. I held up my hand and showed him my ring, not that that was probably a deterrent for someone who was having an affair with a married woman and looking for more on the side.

He shrugged. "If you change your mind, you know where I am. I'm Vince, by the way."

I answered, "Hi, Vince," to be polite. Then I gave him an "I don't think so" smile and took the drinks to where Mum and Imani were sitting. I made a BOS, handed out the drinks, and sat. "Oh my God. What a sleazebag."

Imani smirked. "I thought it looked like he was hitting on you. What a charmer."

"Yeah, who in their right mind would pick Will over him?" I rolled my eyes.

"You could do worse." Mum cocked her head to the side while she regarded him. "Nice brown eyes, thick, dark hair, high cheekbones."

"He's not much taller than me, and he has no class. He thinks he's all that, which is really annoying. Maybe if you're into one-night stands and braggers it'd be fine, but not me. All I can think is ew. And I can't believe you're checking him out."

Mum laughed. "I wouldn't touch him with a ten-foot pole. I was just making a point that he wasn't ugly. Besides, I have to get into the spirit of what I'm going to do."

"Oh?"

"I've decided that I'll butter this one up—we already know he likes older women. How old do you think he is?" Mum asked.

Imani checked him out. "Twenty-seven, tops. And Mrs D must be at least fifty."

"So he'd totally go you, Mum." I laughed. "But then, he

just tried to hit on me, so he's probably into women whatever their age. So what's the new plan?"

Mum stood. "I'm going to pump him for information... um, not *pump*, pump, but you know what I mean."

My mouth dropped open. She wasn't usually crude, at least not the parent I remembered, but then again, I was a lot older now. Maybe I just missed a lot of references when I was younger, or she didn't speak like that in front of me because I was only young? "Mum!"

Imani laughed. "Nice one, Katerina."

"So, as I was saying, I'll flirt with him, keep him distracted, and see what I can find out about Mrs D and her relationship with Mr D. Imani can keep that boy at the front desk occupied, and you can slip into the office. Easy-peasy."

They had the easy jobs. "Yeah, super-duper easy-peasy." Sneaking around wasn't my favourite thing to do. Not only did I hate doing the wrong thing, I was paranoid about getting caught. I needed to have a plan in case I did. Maybe I'd just say I was lost? Gah, why couldn't my brain come up with something better? I tapped my thigh. "None of us are meant to be alone though."

Imani shrugged. "Don't worry, Lily. We're all still in the hotel, and we need to get this done quickly. If anything happens, just scream—that goes for you too, Katerina. If Will says anything later, I'll take the heat." Oh, well. If she was happy to take the blame, who was I to stop her? And it wasn't like we were going to be out of hearing distance of each other.

"Okay. Now, wish me luck." Mum smiled, undid the top two buttons of her summery shirt, and turned. She sauntered —sauntered!—to the bar. Who was this woman, and what had she done with my mother? When she got there, she leaned over the bar, giving him a look down her top.

Imani grinned. "Your mum's got some moves. Look at her work it."

"Mmmhmm, just look. I wish I didn't have to." I stood. "Come on. Let's get this over and done with. I think you should go out and distract that guy first. Get him to look towards the front doors, and I'll slip into that room. If you feel my magic because I have to unlock the door, do something with your magic, too, so he doesn't realise what I'm doing."

"Sounds good. Give me a minute, then come out."

She walked fast, and I lagged behind, giving her time to get the job done. Once I reached the doors, I glanced down the hallway. Impressive. Imani was a fast worker. She had the young man's attention. My heart raced as I left the bar area and moved to the right and the office door. I took my phone out, ready to take a photo, and tried turning the handle with the other hand. It was unlocked! It must be my lucky day.

As I opened the door, my whole body tensed, waiting for someone to call out and ask me what the hell I was doing. But the shout never came, and I slid into the room and closed the door quietly behind me.

The office was typical of any office anywhere, except for the pretty terrazzo floors, and Venetian-glass chandelier hanging in the centre of the room. There were two boring timber desks, each with a black office chair and one guest chair in front of one of the tables. One table was tidy and organised, the other had an array of paper on its surface and two dirty coffee cups.

The urge to check out what was on the tables was strong, but I needed to take the photo first. Maybe Agent Tondato would get a search warrant once they'd spoken to Mrs Dal Lago.

I lifted my phone. "Show me Mr Dal Lago the last time he was here."

The windowless room was lit as it was right now—by the chandelier in the middle of the ceiling. He stood face to face with his wife. She had her hands on her hips as she looked up at him, an annoyed expression twisting her face. His face was red, his eyes shooting daggers. Seemed he was angry. I took a photo of them from the side, capturing both expressions, then I took one of him from the front and one of her. I panned the phone around the room, making sure they'd been alone. Yep.

I spun around and looked at the door. Phew. I hadn't been discovered yet. Time to go since I'd gotten what I'd come here for. But where had he gone after this? I cocked my head to the side. A brown, four-drawer-tall filing cabinet sat against the far wall in front of a door. Interesting. I pointed my phone at it.

Voices sounded outside. The knob on the door behind me rattled. *Crap.*

I turned and looked around the room. To hide or not to hide? Damn. I could make excuses about being here accidentally... maybe. But hiding? There was no way to explain that. Damn it. As the door opened, I did the only thing I could think of and made a doorway around myself.

I sucked in quick breaths as I stepped out into Angelica's reception room. I planted my feet and bent at the waist, putting both hands on my thighs. That had been a close call. Whoever had opened that door would surely know that someone had just cast a spell in there. *Crap, crap, crap, crap.*

I still had my phone in my hand, and I texted Imani to tell her where I was. She would've seen whoever it was coming to the door. Maybe her voice was the one I heard, subtly warning me and distracting whoever was about to come in.

If I travelled back to the hotel now, it might be too obvious when I arrived in the reception room. I was stuck here for a while as I didn't have a key to get in. Luckily, there was a chair in here. I sat and called Mum. "Hey, Mum."

"Lily, why are you calling me?"

"Sorry to interrupt your flirt session, but can you come to Angelica's and bring the key. I'll explain later. I think I need to stay here for an hour or so. Maybe tell Imani where you're going."

She sounded frustrated. "Fine. Can you wait ten minutes? I'll have to get Imani to bring me, or maybe I'll give her the key."

I slapped my head. "Oh, yeah. I forgot. Sorry. I'll wait here for Imani while you enjoy your *date*." Yikes. My mother had no magic and couldn't travel. What a stupid thing to ask her to do. *Idiot, Lily.* "And be careful."

"Thanks, sweetie." She hung up, her voice devoid of remorse. I shook my head and smiled. We were just teasing each other. At least I hoped that's what we were doing. I sat up straight. She wouldn't be flirting with him for real, would she? *No, don't be silly, Lily.* And what if she was? It was none of my business. My father had been dead for a long time. Talk about depressing. My mother could fraternise with whoever she wanted. I didn't have to like it though.

I shook my head and hit the side of it with my palm. *Snap out of it. Your mother deserves all the happiness in the world, and you will support her.* Too right I would... or at least I'd try. And how was Will getting along? Were he and Beren learning anything about Mrs Dal Lago? Had Sarah managed to make it to the interview? Was Angelica okay? My brain was speeding along on a rollercoaster of disaster.

Squirrels. Think of squirrels.

I shut my eyes and thought about squirrels: squirrels scurrying, squirrels eating, squirrels standing on their hind legs, boofy tails twitching as they begged for food. After a while, I opened my eyes and looked at my phone. Only another five minutes and she should be here. It was weird that only six minutes ago, I'd been in Venice, and now I was in Westerham. My life was often like the *Twilight Zone*. It weirded me out, even though I'd been living this life for over a year. Would I ever truly get used to it?

Wanting to deplete my nervous energy, I leaned forward, dropped to the floor, and did some push-ups. Three sets of fifteen should do it, and if Imani wasn't here when I'd finished, I could do some sit-ups. I was in the middle of those sit-ups when Imani came through her portal. She stepped on my ankle, flew forward, and hit the wall palms first. *Slap.*

Sharp pain shot from my ankle up my shin. "Ow!" Oops. I hadn't thought that through.

She spun around and looked down at me as I clutched my throbbing ankle. "What. The. Hell. Are you daft?"

I looked up at her and grimaced. "Ah, yeah. Apparently I am. I forgot you'd need some room. Are you okay?"

"Yes, no thanks to you. I could've broken my nose." She folded her arms. "What in the dickens were you doing anyway?"

I lurched to my feet, gently testing my weight on the sore side. It was going to be okay. Other than slight aching, no real damage had been done. I supposed if it had, Beren would be able to fix it today anyway, but still. When would I stop doing stupid things? "Sit-ups. Burning my nervous energy. You know I don't do waiting very well."

She shook her head. "No, you don't."

"So, what happened? As soon as I heard the voices outside and the doorknob, I was out of there. Who was it?"

"That Isabella woman. She came out of the door from the restaurant, and she was in a hurry. I managed to call out to her, but she wasn't stopping for anything. I think she knew someone was in there."

I swallowed. "Crap. There must've been some kind of alert system or security camera in there. Why the hell didn't I check that first? There's no way I can show my face there now. Is there any way we can find out if it's a camera or something else?"

"I'm waiting for Will to call me with the outcome of the interview. If we're lucky, they'll come back with a warrant, and I can check that room out. If it wasn't a camera, you'll be safe to return. If not…."

I sighed. My first holiday in ages, and now I was going to be banned. Argh! Why did this stuff always happen to me? "I'll just have to find somewhere else to stay. But you need me to look in other rooms."

"Maybe. With a bit of luck, we can dig up some more evidence later today. Who knows? We might get enough to figure out where Angelica is."

"Actually, you should see this. She could be on-site for all we know." I pulled out my phone and brought up the photos I'd taken. I handed it to Imani. "See that door. I wonder where it leads."

"Hmm, interesting. But to be fair, there are probably dozens of rooms we haven't seen. They could've put her in a room in the attic." She handed my phone back and slid hers out of her pocket. "I'm going to call B." She dialled and put the phone on speaker.

He answered quietly. "Hey, Im. Just a sec." There was the sound of a chair scraping on concrete, and voices in the background. After a bit, he spoke again, his voice not full volume, but louder than before. "We're still interviewing the suspect. What's up?"

"Assuming you end up with probable cause, can you make sure you get a search warrant for the whole building? Lil and I are thinking that Angelica might be somewhere in the hotel."

"What makes you think that?"

"Well, we have no other leads right now, so that's where we want to start."

"Makes sense. Okay. I'll see what I can do. She's still denying having anything to do with it, but we've matched her magic signature with one of the three we found on him, and he had a life insurance policy of a hundred thousand euros."

"Oh, wow about the magic signature, not so much about the amount of the insurance. It's not even enough to pay back Lorenzo." Yes, it was Imani's conversation, but I couldn't help it.

"Hey, Lily. Yes, on both counts. Anyway, was there anything else? I don't want to miss anything."

Imani shook her head. "No. That's it. Oh, Lily almost got busted in the hotel office today. We need to know whether there are video cameras in there or not. If there are, there's no way she can come back, and Will might get funny looks from the old lady who works there."

"You talking about Isabella?"

"Yes."

"Okay, noted. I'll get back to you when I know something. Bye."

"Bye."

I sighed.

"What's up?"

"I just thought of something. If Mrs D had help, and

whoever it is knows she's being questioned, they might move Angelica if she is there. We need to go back and search now."

"Dammit. You're right. I can't believe I didn't think of that." She jammed her teeth together and squeezed her eyes shut for a moment. She opened them and blew out a big breath. "I think being on holiday has dulled my edges."

"So how are we going to do this without getting arrested?"

"Let me think." She sat in the chair, leaned back, and got comfortable, then stared at the wall.

Hmm, were the squirrels outside, just a few feet away right now? Had Imani brought the key? Maybe I could go and have a little hangout with them? If only I could understand squirrel speak—they might be able to help us sort this out. I slapped my hands together. That was it! "Hey, Cinnamon and Bagel! You could take them to the hotel, and they could get into the rooms without anyone noticing."

She quickly sat up straight. "You're a genius!" She stood. "Next stop, your brother's place."

I dialled James's number. "Hey, boofhead."

"Hello to you too. What's up? Any news on Angelica?"

"Um, things aren't going too well. We haven't found her yet. It's actually why I'm calling. I need Millicent and the rats."

"Dare I ask why?"

"We think they might be hiding her in the hotel, so we need to look in every room. We don't actually know she's there, but just in case. And the rats are the perfect small creatures to do that without alerting anyone."

"Okay. I'll let Mill know—she's working a case out in the field today."

"This is urgent. We were hoping to go to your place and grab the rats and Millicent right now. We only have about an hour, maybe less before they potentially move her."

"Struth, Lily. You don't make things easy."

"It's not my fault. Jeez."

"I know. Sorry. Anyway, let me go, and I'll get onto Mill ASAP. If I haven't heard back from her in five, I'll let you know. Just wait in my reception room."

"Okay, thanks. Bye." I explained everything to Imani.

"Fingers crossed, then, love."

"Yep. Let's go."

We made our doorways and stepped into James's reception room. I knocked on the door on the off-chance Millicent had ducked home for lunch or to use the toilet. There was nothing worse than having to go in a public toilet. A dog barked and scratched on the other side of the door. "Hey, buddy. It's just Lily."

Imani sat on the love seat. "Looks like she's not home. Do her dogs know how to open the door?"

"I thought I'd try… just in case, and no, they don't."

"Miss Impatient. Now we have to listen to that." The dog kept barking, and another one joined him. Now both my brother's dogs were in on it.

"Oops. Sorry." Just so I wouldn't create more havoc, I sat next to Imani, out of the way in case Millicent stepped through. My phone dinged with a message. I looked at my screen. "It's from Millicent. She can get here soon—she just has to find somewhere private to travel from." I tapped my foot on the ground and tried to tune the barking out. They were loud. My toe tapping didn't work. Funny that. I raised my voice to be heard over the dogs. "Wanna play I spy?"

Imani threw me an unimpressed gaze. "Are you serious? There's like five things in here."

"We could pretend we're in the bar at the hotel and do stuff that was in there."

"Has anyone ever told you that you're weird."

"Yes… frequently… many people." I grinned. "Being weird, impatient, and easily surprised are my three biggest skills."

A brief vibration of magic tickled my scalp, and Millicent stepped through her doorway. "Hey, ladies. Sorry you had to wait with all that noise." I stood, and we hugged.

"The noise is my fault. I knocked to check if you were home. Big mistake."

She laughed. "We really should train them better. I've had that conversation with them before, but they don't listen… obviously. Anyway, come in. I understand it's urgent." She unlocked the door, and the dogs stopped barking, but they did jump up on Millicent. "Get down."

"Yes. Super urgent." I gave both dogs a quick pat on the head.

Imani came in and shut the reception-room door. "We need to get back to the hotel ASAP. I was hoping you and the rats could come with me. I don't want Lily there right now, just in case she's been compromised. She might have been caught by a security camera snooping in the hotel office."

Millicent frowned as she continued through kitchen and into the family room. "What do you need? I'll convey it to the rats." She walked to the corner where there was a plywood box with a doorway cut into it. "Cinnamon, Bagel. I need your help."

Imani explained the plan as my cute little friends exited their sleeping quarters. I grinned and sat on the floor. "Hello, you two!" They scurried to me and squeaked. I patted each of them on the back. "How have you been?"

Millicent smiled. "They say they've been good and that they miss you—you don't come over enough."

"Sorry. I've been making the most of being able to go out again, and we're supposed to be on holiday. Anyway, it's great to see you." Bagel climbed up my shorts and top, then up to my shoulder. Her favourite spot. She nuzzled into my neck.

"Okay, ladies, pay attention." I looked up, but silly me. Millicent was talking to the rats, not me. She told them what we wanted them to do. "They say they're happy to help."

"I knew we could count on you guys. Thank you." I stroked Bagel's back.

"Squeak, squeak."

I looked to Millicent for a translation. "She said always." Millicent picked up Cinnamon. "Now that's organised, I guess I should dress for a Venetian holiday."

"Are you sure I shouldn't come? Maybe I could be a big distraction for the old woman? She could get angry at me while you two are checking out all the rooms."

Imani bit her bottom lip and held it there for a moment. "Hmm. Tell you what. We'll go without you, but if we need a decoy, I'll text you 'yes,' and you come to the reception room, then try and keep her there as long as possible… using non-violent means." She gave me a stern look.

"Oh my God. As if I'd do anything to forcibly keep her there. I don't want to end up in jail. I figured she could interrogate me about why I was in the office. I could string that out for ages." I was queen of the confusing conversation. Ooh, a fourth skill.

Imani looked at me for a while, likely thinking. She finally said, "That could work." She looked at Millicent, who had magicked a pretty summer dress on—it was white with a small-blue-flower print. It had two big pockets at thigh level, and she slipped Cinnamon into one and Bagel into the other.

Millicent smiled. "Ready to roll."

Imani made a doorway. "After you." Millicent stepped through, and Imani followed. The doorway shut, leaving me alone. Well, Millicent's two dogs were here, but I was practically alone. Now all I had to do was wait.

And we all knew how good I was at doing that.

CHAPTER 7

My phone rang. It had only been about five minutes since they'd left. Had they already found something? Heart racing, I slid my phone out of my pocket.

Damn.

Unknown number.

Now was not the time to be getting a sales call from some company who wanted to sell me ink cartridges, or from someone telling me the "police" were after me for avoiding taxes. Just in case it was important—maybe Will was calling me from the PIB Trieste office—I pressed the answer button. "Hello?" I braced myself to hang up quickly if it was a scammer. Normally, I'd love to keep them on the phone and pretend to believe them to waste their time, but I wasn't in the mood.

"Hello, Miss Bianchi?" The woman on the other end sounded familiar and had an Italian accent.

Who could it be? I wasn't answering till I knew. I mean,

why did people do this? Call someone and ask who they were before saying who the caller was. *Excuse me, but you're calling me, bucko.* "Who is this?"

She tittered. "*Mi Scusi*! It is Isabella from the 'otel. I was wondering if you could come and join me for a coffee. The camera, it showed you were in the 'otel office. I'd like to know why."

Crap. What the hell should I do now? What if I admitted it, and she had me arrested? Well, it's not like they could arrest me while I was in the UK, but it meant I couldn't go back to Venice... ever. And she was a fairly nice old lady who was going through enough right now with the murder of her boss. Maybe she'd forgive me if she knew why I was looking? "Sorry. I was just trying to find some information. My dear friend Angelica has gone missing, and I've been looking everywhere. She has a habit of drinking too much and falling asleep in weird places. I thought maybe she had accidentally gone in there and, you know, fallen asleep." What was a lie between strangers?

"Mio Dio!" Silence for a bit. "I'm so sorry." She sighed, and her voice sounded worn down, tired. "All the things happening here. Evil is around. First, my son-in-law is murdered, and they think my beautiful Elena has killed him. I know she would not. She is a good girl, and she loved him. And now your friend is missing. What are we going to do? Who will be next?" Were they sniffles I could hear on the other end?

Wow, she was the suspect's mother? No wonder she was upset. Hmm, I debated her claim that her daughter loved him. Elena didn't love him enough to either break it off with him or not see other men, even though it broke his heart. "It's okay,

Isabella. I'm sure Angelica will turn up soon. Are you going to be all right?"

"I don't know. Oh, Miss Bianchi. I'm very worried. I don't feel well. My daughter is with those agents, and my grandson is out. What should I do?"

Damn it. My conscience knew what the right thing to do was. At least I could legitimately go back there without getting in trouble. "Why don't I come and have that coffee with you until you feel a bit better? I'm not busy at the moment. I can stay till your grandson gets back."

"Oh, would you? Grazie, grazie."

"I'll see you in a minute." I hung up and sighed. Now it was going to be awkward when Imani and Millicent messaged or called. I couldn't very well say too much in front of Isabella. Well, at least I'd be doing my job and distracting the old lady. Maybe this would work in our favour. Who woulda thunk it? The universe was playing nice for a change. Although what would it ask in return?

I made my doorway to the hotel reception room and stepped through. I didn't even have to buzz because Isabella was waiting for me. She had a white apron on over her pink-red-and-white floral-printed dress. She slapped her hands on her cheeks, and a look of relief washed over her face, although it did nothing to erase the dark circles under her eyes. "Grazie, grazie! I'm so glad you came. I wasn't happy when I saw you in the office camera, but I understand now." She shook her head. "I just don't know what to do. I've been cooking to, how you say, not think of my sadness, and also, with Antonio gone, we have more work to do. This could not have happened at a worse time. The 'otel, she is almost full at the moment. Finally, after a quiet winter." She seemed to come to, her eyes widening. "Forgive me. Please, come and have coffee and *zaleti*. I baked it today."

Mmm. I could never turn down a dessert, especially a homemade one, well, assuming zaleti was a dessert. The word baking had been used, so I assumed the best. "That would be lovely. Thank you." As we walked down the hallway and through to the dining room, I couldn't help listening for Imani and Millicent, or glancing around. Which part of the hotel were they in? Were they having any luck? How long would it take to find Angelica?

My stomach twisted, and the urge for dessert deserted me. I was even too stressed to laugh at the similarity of dessert and desert. As we entered the restaurant, the fragrance wafting out of the kitchen sent my tastebuds into a frenzy. "That smells delicious."

She smiled. "I love to cook. I'm preparing tonight's menu. Our two most popular food is *bigoli in salsa* and *fegato alle Venez-ian*." I had no idea what they were, but they smelled divine.

"Maybe I should book a table for tonight. I'd love to try them." Would we be eating dinner like normal people tonight, or would we be in a frenzy of searching for Angelica? I couldn't see any of us having much of an appetite if she was still missing, or even worse, if we found her body. *Argh, do not go there, Lily!*

She led me to a table for two near the kitchen door. "Sit, please." She smiled, and once I was seated, she disappeared through the swinging door to the kitchen.

I gazed around the restaurant. Maroon carpet, tables set with thick, clean white tablecloths. Small vases with flowers sat in the middle of each table—it was all very quaint. It looked like a lot of work, but for a witch establishment, it would've all happened with a thought. Come to think of it, why was she physically cooking and not magicking it? Maybe her magic was even weaker than her daughter's and it was too tiring, especially since she was cooking for a lot of people?

She returned to the table with the best-smelling coffee ever and a dinner plate full of what must be zaleti. I'd never heard of them before, but I was game. They were diamond-shaped, yellowish biscuits with icing sugar sprinkled on top. "Thank you." I took one and put it on the small plate that had already been on the table when I sat. I inhaled the coffee steam through my nose before I sipped it. The taste dazzled my tongue, and then the warmth travelled down my throat. "Ahhhh. Wonderful. Grazie." I enjoyed using what little Italian I knew, plus it was probably nice for my host that I tried to dabble in her language.

"*Prego.*"

I bit into the cookie and chewed. "Mmm. That's different. Oh, are those raisins?"

"Si. They are soaked in liquor first." She winked. Shame cooking them would kill the alcohol. Not that I was desperate for a drink. The clearer my head, the better right now.

My phone dinged. I looked at Isabella, hoping the unease snaking through my belly wasn't showing on my face. Had they found something? I smiled awkwardly. "Sorry. I just need to check this… just in case it's about Angelica." I carefully looked at my phone, making sure I was the only one who could see the screen. It was from Imani.

So far, nothing. We've looked in all the rooms on our floor and the floor above, although three were occupied. When we explained we were looking for a friend, they were happy to let us look inside. We might need your distraction soon. Heading to the top floor now. Be on the ground floor in five minutes. Can you come then?

I responded. *Already here. In restaurant having coffee with*

Isabella. I'll keep her occupied. The little dots moved, indicating Imani was typing something. They stopped, started, stopped. I chuckled. I'd surprised her, and she was likely wondering how the hell I was in the situation I was in. She'd have to wait. Finally, her response came through.

??? Okay. You can explain later. Bye. I slid my phone back in my pocket.

"Is everything all right?" Isabella asked.

I gave her a sad smile. "I guess so. My friend hasn't found Angelica yet. She was just checking where I was. I told her I was here, having coffee with you." She nodded, and something I couldn't read flashed across her eyes. She placed a hand on her forehead and shut her eyes. I leaned forward. "Are you all right, Isabella?"

"My head. It is spinning. Sleeping… is hard since my son-in-law was killed." Her eyes opened, and I was pretty sure it was fear shining from them. "What if someone wants to kill all of us? Enrico owed lots of money to that 'orrible man at the glass factory. My daughter told me he threatened her over the telephone… before Antonio was killed." Oh, crap. Had we discounted the killer?

"What did he say? Do you know?"

She shook her head. "She said she didn't want to upset me, but she told Antonio, and he was going to fix it…." She looked at the ceiling, then back at me. "He didn't fix it very well."

I frowned. "Apparently not." My head throbbed, and I rubbed my forehead. Just what I needed—a headache. I downed the rest of my espresso—the coffee was smooth and rich, but I still preferred my cappuccinos. I had a feeling that espressos were the coffee of choice for Italians, and I hadn't wanted to trouble Isabella.

My phone rang. I jumped in my seat. *Dammit, Lily. Stop*

being shocked at the smallest sound. I answered it. I breathed out in relief at Will's name on the screen. I looked at Isabella. "Sorry. I have to take this." She waved me to take it. I answered the phone. "Hey, what's happening?"

"Things are becoming more complicated."

I scrunched my forehead. "What do you mean?"

"We've found out about Lorenzo Zanini's threat to Mrs Dal Lago. And Agent Tondato has proof that the alibi was manufactured. We'll be back there in minutes, and so will Mrs Dal Lago. Whatever you've got going on, you need to stop now. Mrs Dal Lago has said we can have a look for Angelica. She claims she has nothing to hide."

I sagged, whether in disappointment or relief, I didn't know. There wasn't anything I could explain to Will, so I just said goodbye and hung up. At least Isabella would feel better soon, when her daughter came home. "Thank you for the coffee and food. Are you feeling any better?"

She shrugged and stroked the plait that sat over her shoulder and fell to her lap. "Maybe a little. Will you stay with me a while longer?" I couldn't ignore that puppy-dog-pleading look that radiated from her eyes.

I smiled. "Sure."

She placed her soft, wrinkled hand over mine on the table, and as much as I wanted to pull away—touching strangers was so ridiculously awkward—I stayed where I was because let it not be said that I disappointed old people who were going through a tough time.

Thankfully, Will must have called Imani and explained the situation because within two minutes, she walked through the restaurant door. "Lily! There you are. I've been looking for you everywhere."

Before I could stand and greet her, Mrs Dal Lago hurried

through the door and came straight to our table, her face troubled. "Mama!" She said something in Italian, her hands waving. Isabella stood slowly and embraced her daughter. I had no idea what they were saying to each other, but at least I was free to leave and not be touched.

I went to Imani and made a bubble of silence. "Apparently we're allowed to search for Angelica."

"I heard. Will and B are already here. They've gone straight to the office—they want you to meet them there."

"Okay. Also, we need to check on Mum." I dropped the BOS and was about to say goodbye to Isabella, but she and her daughter were arguing, voices raised. Her daughter planted her hands on her hips. Her mother jerked her chin up and waved a finger at her. What was harder to understand than Italian? Italian when two people were yelling over the top of each other. To interrupt or not to interrupt. Imani and I shared a double eyebrow raise. Hmm, one of us should be recording this. I pulled my phone out again, found the recording app, and pressed record. Unfortunately, I only managed to get a minute of it before Isabella stared at me, her tirade fading away. Her daughter turned towards us, likely to see what her mother was looking at.

I smiled. "Sorry to interrupt. We're going to go now and look for Angelica."

Both women nodded, and Isabella managed a small smile. "Thank you for staying with me."

"It was my pleasure. I hope you're both going to be okay."

Her daughter sent a glare my way. "We will be fine. Thank you." Ooooooookay. Maybe we weren't welcome in this establishment anymore. Will had helped interrogate her after all. But if we changed hotels, we'd be less likely to get to the bottom of this disaster.

"Okay. Ciao." I waved, and Imani and I hurried out. As soon as we were in the hallway, I stopped recording. "I'll need to get this to Mum, see what they were saying." It struck me that I hadn't seen her since I'd returned. "Let's check the bar. And where's Millicent?"

"She's got the rats. Since we're allowed to look through things now, she went home. She's in the middle of a case, don't forget."

"I know. Bummer. Stupid PIB."

"Hey, watch it."

"Sorry. I would've said that about any work that would keep her from looking for Angelica." I had a way of putting my foot in my mouth when I least expected it. Another one of my many talents.

We checked the bar, and my mother was still there, sitting on a barstool, gazing into the bartender's eyes. He was laughing, maybe at something my mother had said. I went up to her. "Hello, Lily." She smiled.

"Just checking up on you. How's it going?"

"Oh, great thanks. How about you?" Well, she was giving nothing away.

"I need to talk to you about something. Could you come outside for a sec?"

"Of course!" She turned back to the bartender. "I'm sorry I have to go, but it was lovely chatting with you."

He grinned. "Of course. Come and chat with me any time. I would love to have you." He winked. I suppressed a gag.

Mum slid off the stool and joined us in the hall. I made a bubble of silence and put on an Italian accent in a deep voice. "I would love to have you?!"

She giggled. "I know. His flirting game needs some work. He's harmless though. So, what did you find?"

I sighed. "Not much, but I took a recording of the end of an argument between Isabella and her daughter."

"And I've checked most of the rooms with Millicent, and we found nothing."

My mother's face fell. "Oh. That's not promising."

I shook my head. "No. It's not. And keeping Will's rule in mind, do you want to come with us to check out the office?"

"Okay. Lead the way. I might just stand at the door so I'm not underfoot."

"That's okay. Whatever makes you happy." I smiled.

We turned and in a few steps were at the office. The door was open, so Imani and I went straight in. Will, Beren, and Agent Tondato were there. Beren was looking through paperwork on the messy desk while Agent Tondato went through drawers of the filing cabinet that sat in front of the door I wanted to check behind. Will stood in the middle of the room, his power glowing around him as his magic tickled my scalp. "What are you doing?" I asked.

He looked at me, poker face intact. "Just checking for any anomalies that would indicate a hidden room."

A pointed at the door behind the filing cabinet. "Don't look now, but there's a door."

Will rolled his eyes. "Very funny."

"She hasn't been in here. I couldn't sense her earlier, and I can't now." I was being subtle, but he would know I meant I hadn't captured her in my camera. "But I sense Mr Dal Lago was here the day he was murdered." Will knew I had the photo of him going through that doorway.

Agent Tondato, who was sitting on an office chair, looked

up at me from the drawer he was rifling through. "Do you have a special talent for sensing where people have been?"

"Yes."

"I've heard anyone with that talent is limited to maybe twelve hours after the person was there." I shrugged, trying to keep the stories to a minimum. The more embellished the lie was, the more likely I'd be caught out. "So, maybe you're making an educated guess since you saw him come out of this office after arguing with his wife."

"*While* arguing with his wife." I folded my arms and clenched my teeth. I so wanted to say to Imani, see he hates me, but that was way too childish. "And my statement is not a guess. It's a fact." Sticking out my tongue would also be childish, but my tongue managed to make it halfway out of my mouth before I caught it and pretended to be licking my lips. Oh, great; now he'd think I was flirting.

He looked at Will. "Do you always let your fiancée follow you on investigations?"

He turned his poker face onto the agent—I guessed he couldn't look angry, or we might get no more cooperation from him. "She's very skilled at sensing things. She's helped the PIB solve many cases. If it wasn't for Lily, there would be a lot more witch criminals running around out there." He turned to me and gave a small smile. I gave him a thank-you nod and smile in return.

Agent Tondato flicked his gaze to Imani, then back to Will. "Women should not be in the field. It is too dangerous, and they're not as good as male agents. The women miss things." Oh, dear. He'd just about signed his own death warrant. I looked at Imani and noted sparks of anger shooting from her eyes. It was a miracle the Italian agent didn't catch fire, or at least complain that his skin was burning.

Imani opened her mouth to say something, but Will raised a brow. It must be a reminder that we needed to find Angelica, and we could deal with this idiot later. She shut her mouth, but her nostrils flared a few times. She really had some fierce self-control. It was a shame I didn't.

I looked down my nose at him. "Considering most men can't find what's right in front of their nose in the cupboard or fridge, I think you mean we're way better than men. When was the last time you had to ask your mother to find something for you?" Imani snorted. I smiled, happy I'd made her feel better. Unfortunately, the same couldn't be said for Will, who gave me a dirty "shut up" look.

Agent Tondato pressed his lips together and lifted his chin. "My mumma is excellent at finding things in the house, yes, but that is all. A man's intellect is more suited to important things."

My mouth dropped open, but before anything could come flying out, Will stepped between Agent Tondato and me. He was looking at the Italian agent. "Do you think you could avoid insulting my colleagues? You may do things differently here, but I can assure you that our female agents do as good a job as our male agents. If we can just stick to the case and find Angelica and the murderer, I would very much appreciate it. I wouldn't want to have to involve UK headquarters—Angelica is one of their top agents. If they think you've botched things up, they might just convince the powers that be to take away funding for your branch."

Wow, Will was getting serious. He wasn't usually into threats… well, at least not that I'd seen. And how did that work anyway, with the international agencies? I knew funding for the UK arm was being squeezed, but did funding for other countries' agencies come from different sources?

Agent Tondato didn't say anything, but he gave a nod, his face pinched. Right, hopefully we'd be on track to get this place searched. The worry worm in my stomach kept burrowing. We needed to find Angelica today. "Can we move that cabinet and search in there?"

Will turned and looked at me. "Of course." He turned back to the filing cabinet, and his magic tickled my skull. The cabinet disappeared, then reappeared in the opposite corner of the office. Agent Tondato gave Will an annoyed look—he'd been going through that filing cabinet. The Italian agent stood and pushed his wheeled chair to the other side of the room to continue exploring the cabinet's contents.

I smiled at Will. "Thank you."

"My pleasure." Will placed his hand on his stomach and half bowed. He turned, went to the door, and tried the knob. It was locked. Another tingle of his magic, and the knob turned. My heart thudded, the beat playing in my ears. Was Angelica behind there? He donned a return to sender and opened the door, all of us staring at it... waiting. The urge to bite my fingernails was strong.

Darkness filled the doorframe. Will felt around on the other side of the wall, then *click*. Light shone from the room. Agent Tondato, maybe satisfied that nothing was going to come through that door, turned back to the drawer he was going through. That suited me—now I could join Will in the other room and take some photos.

Will slipped into the room. Imani and I followed. Once we were away from Tondato's critical gaze, I slid my phone out and brought up the camera app. Before I asked anything, I gazed around the windowless space. The floor was the same orangey-brown terrazzo as the rest of the hotel. Another filing cabinet sat in one corner, next to a row of boxes piled two high that ran the length of one wall. The musty and slightly pungent odour of damp thickened the air.

Will turned to Imani. "If you can look for any magic signatures, that would be great. I'm going to look for any physical signs, and our little Aussie can do her thing."

I saluted. "Yes, sir!" He rolled his eyes. I smirked. He hated when I pretended to obey him. Time to get to work. I lifted my phone and drew magic. "Show me Angelica," I whispered. Might as well get straight to the point.

I sucked in a breath. My stomach plunged. She lay on a dirty mattress in front of the boxes, eyes closed, hands and feet bound. Was she still alive? I walked closer and snapped off two shots. Her lips were pink, not blue, and there was no blood that I could see. Hopefully that boded well. I swallowed and lowered the phone before raising it again. "Show me who brought Angelica here." Nothing. What the hell? "Argh!"

Imani jerked her gaze towards me. "What's wrong?" Concern laced her voice.

I showed her the photos. "When I asked who did it, no one showed up."

Will stood behind Imani and looked over her shoulder. He ran a hand through his hair, and his poker face slipped for a moment, revealing the worry underneath. "So, they magicked her here?"

"I guess. Hang on. Let me try something else. If they put her here, they might have also put Mr D here physically rather than magically." I lifted the camera and whispered, "Show me the last time Mr Dal Lago was here and who he was here with."

Just like with Angelica, or not quite, he was unconscious or already dead, hands and feet bound, but he was lying on the hard floor rather than a mattress. Whoever killed him, really didn't like him. Although, if he were already dead, he wouldn't feel the discomfort of being on the concrete. I took a photo and showed Will and Imani.

"Well, that's good," said Imani. "They had a beef with him, but she's just getting in the way. Maybe she found a clue where they found the old-lady victim?"

I shook my head. "But how would the killer even know what Angelica found? It's not like she would've called or texted anyone."

Will shrugged. "Maybe Angelica asked our killer a question that made them balk, or maybe the killer was at the scene of the crime, watching the investigators?"

I sighed. "Well, whatever it is, Angelica's no longer here, so that sucks. Now what?"

Will straightened his shoulders. "We keep looking."

We left Agent Tondato in the office. Beren got Liv to come down from their room. She and my mother joined us as we went from room to room, until we'd covered all the guest accommodation—for the second time—storage rooms, and offices. But no luck. We reconvened in the hallway outside the office. By then, Agent Tondato had already left, but he hadn't bothered texting Will to let him know. Had he found anything worthwhile?

Will turned to my mother. "Did you get any info from your chat with the bartender?"

"I don't know. I just need to ruminate on my conversation with Mrs D's boyfriend. Most of it was him complaining that even though Mr D is dead, Mrs D won't commit to being exclusive with him. I asked if she ever promised to leave her husband for him, and he said no."

"What's his alibi?" I asked because, surely the dead man's wife's lover was a suspect.

"He was here working." Will nodded towards the bar. "Security footage confirms he was there until closing at midnight. He has an apartment nearby. We have footage of him leaving here and then not returning."

"The Italian agents have pretty much cleared him," said Beren. Oh, great, so all that cloak and daggers stuff, getting my mum to flirt with him, was all for nothing. "Turns out that Mrs Dal Lago's magic signature was one of the two on her husband we couldn't identify, but she claims it was from restraining him in the bedroom that morning, and it was consensual."

"How are you supposed to prove that?" Seemed like Mrs D had all her bases covered. "She sure had an active sex life. Maybe she has one of those sex disorders?"

Imani raised her brows. "How many sex disorders are there, love?"

"How the hell am I supposed to know? Probably thousands, but I mean the one where you just can't get enough. Maybe she wasn't trying to hurt her husband—maybe he just couldn't perform as much as she needed him to? It's still no excuse, but it takes away her motive. Have you had her assessed by a psychologist?"

Will stared at me as if I'd lost the plot. "Lily, you know we haven't. We've barely been able to get a search warrant on this place. And just because she enjoys lots of sex, doesn't mean she has a disorder... necessarily."

"Yes, but it was her idea to have an open marriage, and from what I saw, he was upset about it, and if she truly loved him, she'd keep it on the down-low, but she didn't. I figure it's because she just can't help herself when the urge strikes."

"Or she's a bi—"

"Now, now, Imani, let's not use that language here." Beren

looked around, his gaze hitting Isabella, who'd apparently been listening from the doorway to the restaurant. Gah, why hadn't we used a BOS? Being on holiday had turned us into a bunch of amateurs.

Isabella's gaze met mine, and I gave her an "I'm sorry" look. She blinked, her eyes watering, and her head slowly fell forward. She turned and slunk back into the restaurant. I wanted to run after her, but it wasn't the time—she might have been upset, but so were we. "I think we just made a mess of that."

My mother sighed. "You lot should know better than that. If Angelica were here, she'd be ropable."

My cheeks heated. There were only two people who could make me feel such mortifying guilt—Angelica and my mother. It was like being ten again. Will kept his gaze on my mother, an apology in his eyes. Imani and I looked at each other. I was betting from the awkward look on her face that her shame matched mine. We totally should've known better. Thank God Millicent wasn't here to see this. Liv and Beren were the only ones who could look at my mother without a thick layer of chagrin clogging their pores.

"You're right." My tone couldn't have been any more apologetic than it was. "I think we're all just a bit put out. We're worried about Angelica… but that's no excuse. Sorry."

"Yes, love, I'm sorry too."

"Me three," said Will. I guessed this was his future mother-in-law, and other than being a nice guy, he probably didn't want to put a dent in their shiny new relationship.

My mother gave us all a firm parental stare. "Do better next time." She looked at Beren. "Can you please make a bubble of silence?"

"I'd be glad to." Beren's magic tickled my scalp, and it was done.

Something I'd wondered but hadn't had a chance to ask pinged in my brain. "Where's Sarah and Lavender, and, Mum, can you translate this please?" I brought up the recording on my phone while Will answered my first question.

"They had to get back straight after the interview. They're working this evening, but they'll join us again after dinner."

"Okay, thanks." I looked at Mum. "What are they saying?" I pressed Play on the recording, and Isabella's and her daughter's voices filled our bubble.

When it was done, Mum frowned. "Can you play it again? My Italian's not the best, and we don't have the beginning of the conversation."

"Okay." I played it two more times.

"I think Isabella is telling her daughter the police are stupid for accusing her and not to tell them anything. She also told her to stop sleeping around. Her daughter basically told her to keep her opinions to herself. It wouldn't hurt to ask Sarah to listen to it. She'll be able to get more out of it, maybe."

"Thanks." I really needed to get to it on the other languages. I hated not understanding stuff. "In any case, we know someone in this hotel put Angelica in that room."

My mother's face paled. "What are you talking about?"

Beren's brow wrinkled. "Yes, what *are* you talking about?"

"Oh, I'm sorry. Mum, you were standing out here when I found it, and B was in the office with Agent Tondato—I couldn't show him without revealing my secret."

Beren gave a nod. "So show me now."

"Gladly." I brought up the photo and handed it to Beren.

Liv stood on one side of him, and Mum moved to stand on his other side.

Liv sucked in a breath. "Is she...?"

Will cleared his throat. "Dead? No, we don't think so. She has normal colouring. That either means she was only just killed when she was transported there, or she's still alive. It's impossible to know for sure, but we're betting she's alive."

Mum put her fingers to her temples. "You're right, Lily. Someone from this hotel is the most likely to have done this. Which brings us back to Mrs D."

The front door to the hotel opened, and a large man walked through. Oh, boy. This was interesting. "Or someone who knows the place well...."

Everyone turned to see what I was looking at.

Lorenzo Zanini halted and stared at us. Beren canned the BOS, and Will spoke. "What are you doing here?"

"Elena called me."

I raised a brow. "Mrs Dal Lago?"

"Yes." He folded his arms—so defensive. Was she seeing him too? Sheesh, the plot was thicker than a well-cooked risotto. Mmm, risotto. My stomach gurgled. Must be time to eat. Should we eat out, or should we eat here so we could try and get some more info out of Isabella? She was all for her daughter, but maybe she'd noticed something that didn't seem like a clue to her but that we could use. Maybe I could frame it as I was trying to clear her daughter? Gah, liar, liar pants on fire. Although, if she was innocent, I did want to prove it. The only way we'd find Angelica was if we figured out who the guilty person was.

"Why?" asked Will.

The glass-blower narrowed his eyes. "None of your business. Excuse me." He let his arms drop to his sides, and he stomped past us to the restaurant.

I looked at Will. "Can't you stop him?"

He shook his head. "No. He hasn't been arrested, even though he's still a person of interest." This was doing my head in.

"But wasn't his alibi found to be BS?"

My mother's mouth fell open. "Lily! Manners, please."

I smirked. "What's wrong with bullishly shoddy?"

She shook her head, and Imani snickered. Imani mouthed, *Nice save.* I grinned.

Beren made another bubble of silence. "While we're out here talking rubbish, he's in there talking to Mrs Dal Lago. Why don't we see if we can listen in?" Will gave a nod, and Beren dropped the BOS. Will's magic tickled my scalp, and white noise reached us.

I scrunched my brow. "What's that?"

The white noise stopped, and Will frowned. "They must have erected a bubble of silence. Damn it."

I blew an irritated breath out of my nose. "We have to hurry. Whoever did this could vanish at any moment, never to be seen again, and we'll never find out where Angelica is."

Movement at the door to the restaurant caught my eye. Isabella was holding onto the bellboy's arm— Francesco if I remembered correctly—as he tried to attack Lorenzo. Then Elena grabbed Francesco's other arm and looked apologetically at Lorenzo. Isabella's raspy voice was louder than a normal conversational tone but not exactly shouting. She was trying to get the young man to see reason, if her facial expression was anything to go by.

Even though the group knew we were there, in the rush of the argument, they must've forgotten, but now they realised.

Isabella, Elena, and Lorenzo turned to frown at us, but Francesco kept glaring at his foe. What the hell was going on? Was Lorenzo trying to get the money out of them? But if that was the case, why would Elena ask him to come over?

Throbbing materialised in my forehead. Just what I needed: a headache. My stomach grumbled loudly, likely agreeing with me. It was as if my talkative tummy had broken the freeze spell, and Lorenzo's gaze flicked to me before he looked at Elena. Something passed between them—it wasn't anger... maybe an apology? Mrs D gave a slow nod, and Lorenzo made a doorway, then left.

Isabella yanked Francesco, freeing him from Elena's grip. She said something to her daughter and dragged the young man away with her. What the hell was that all about? Was Elena trying to sleep with him too? Elena's shoulders dropped, and she sighed heavily. In that moment, rather than looking like a put-together, gorgeous Italian lady about town, she looked tired, exhausted, even heartsore. Her gaze met mine. She shook her head, made a doorway, then left.

And after all that drama, we didn't know much more than when we started, plus Angelica was still missing.

I sighed.

Wow, what an awesome holiday this was turning out to be.

CHAPTER 8

That evening, we opted for an early dinner so we could get back to investigating. My stomach cheered at the suggestion, even though not knowing where Angelica was dampened my appetite. Investigating on an empty stomach was a terrible idea. I'd only have half my brain on the job; the other half would be consoling my grumbling stomach. We found a small, quiet restaurant not far from the hotel. We could've eaten in the hotel, but we all needed a break from the scene of the crime.

After our mains were delivered—the pasta marinara I ordered was the best I'd ever tasted—we got to talking. Will cast a partial bubble of silence—it meant people at nearby tables could hear us, but anyone trying to listen in with magic couldn't. It would've looked totally weird if we were talking and no noise was happening. We checked out the staff and the six other diners in there, confirming they were all non-witches. As a result of this, we kept our voices as low as possible.

Sarah was sitting on one side of me, Will the other. I

handed Sarah my phone so she could listen to the recording from earlier. When she was done, she handed it back. "Isabella told her daughter she knows she's innocent and not to tell the police anything. She also chastised her for sleeping around. Elena told her to mind her own business and that she'll do as she pleases."

My mum looked at her from across the table. "So you're confirming what I thought. Unfortunately, it doesn't give us much to work with." Her gaze shifted to me. "If only you'd started recording earlier." She gave me a sympathetic look. "But don't worry. It's better than nothing."

"I know. I'm a bit slow sometimes, but we are supposed to be on holidays. I'm not as on the ball as usual."

Will rubbed my back. "It's okay, Lily. You more than made up for that by taking those photos. At least we have something."

I stabbed a mussel with my fork. "Yes, but that something isn't helping us find her. There's so much we don't know." I lifted my head to meet Will's gaze. "Why was that other woman murdered? Why did Lorenzo lie about where he was that night? Where is Angelica, and why did someone take her? And what is all that drama with Francesco and Isabella?"

Imani, who was sitting opposite me, next to Mum, furrowed her brow. "Gee, love, when you put it like that, we might as well pull up stumps and go home."

"I'm not saying that. It's just…. We need to do more, think harder. I'd like to sneak back to Lorenzo's factory and take more photos. There were parts of the property we didn't have access to."

Lavender dabbed his mouth with his cloth napkin. "Does he live there?"

"No," said Will. "When he was initially a suspect, they

inspected his apartment and found no evidence of anything untoward."

I rested my fork on my bowl. "Seriously? Does this mean we have another place to check out? We can't leave anything unexplored. If only this had happened in the UK." Or, rather, if only this hadn't happened at all. My shoulders slumped.

Beren's eyes radiated understanding. "I know, Lily, but it didn't, and we're just going to have to deal. But I have faith in us, and Angelica would too." Yeah, that was if she was still alive. I didn't voice what everyone was likely thinking—it would serve no purpose except to depress everyone further. Except, we hadn't found her made into glass anywhere, so that gave me hope, and I would cling to that hope until I knew otherwise.

I tapped my fingers on the table, then sat up straighter. "What if we waited until dark tonight and checked out his factory; then tomorrow, when he's at work, we break into his apartment?"

My mother stared at me. "You can't break into someone's home, Lily. That's illegal."

"Angelica's life is in massive danger. What happened to your adventurous spirit, Mum? I'd be happy to risk jail time to look for evidence. What if he's since moved her there? Maybe she was still in that room behind the office, and after he was sure the police were done with his apartment, he sent her there?"

"*If* he's the guilty party." My mother took a deep breath. "Look, Lily, I'm sorry I can't be happy for you to jump into something that could land you in jail. Being locked up is no picnic." A haunted look invaded her eyes.

"Argh! I'm so sorry. I know you've suffered, but this is different. At least if I'm incarcerated, you guys can still visit.

Besides, I've done jail time before. Relieving myself in front of people wasn't much fun, I'll admit, but I can handle it."

My mother's mouth fell open. "What?! Why were you in jail?" I briefly explained what had happened when I'd first gone to Westerham to help look for James. She gave Will and Beren dirty looks. "How could you not trust Lily? What's wrong with you lot?"

Will swallowed. "Um…. We didn't not trust her, but we hardly knew her. We were just doing our jobs. To be fair, Angelica was running the show. You might want to have a word with her too."

"Mum, it's fine. It's water under the bridge. The point is, I'd risk that to save Angelica. We can't afford to muck around."

"How do we know she hasn't already been turned to glass?" Liv asked. My stomach dropped.

Imani placed her fork on her plate. "Because whoever it was would've displayed her somewhere by now. The only thing we should be worried about is if they chose to just kill her the normal way."

"But why do that when he or she has shown off their other two 'sculptures.'" I shuddered.

Mum drained her wine glass. "I've changed my mind. You need to get into his place as quickly as possible."

I blinked. She'd changed direction like an unpredictable kangaroo on a roadway. One minute they're bounding along-side you, and the next they're in front of your car. "What?"

"I think whoever it is, especially if it's that Lorenzo fellow, will turn her to glass—imagine the ego trip of besting a PIB agent, especially when they've put you in jail before. The thing is, whoever did it is probably out of the power they need. It would take some recovering from that level of power usage, and they didn't just change one person, but two people. We might only have a few hours, or we might have another day, but we're running out of time for sure now."

"So, are we assuming Lorenzo did it, but do we think Mrs Dal Lago helped?" I wanted to get this straight. We were jumping to conclusions, but lying about his whereabouts on the night Angelica went missing and having close ties to the family meant that other than Mrs D, he was the most likely suspect.

Will nodded. "Yes. I think Mrs Dal Lago had something to do with it, even if it's just giving Lorenzo access to the hotel on the night or being an accessory. I don't like that we haven't proven this beyond a reasonable doubt, but, hopefully, further investigation will get us the answers we need."

"Right," said Imani. "What's the plan?"

Once it was dark, Will and I left the hotel. We'd dressed in black clothes and baseball caps. The less people could describe about us later, the better. We donned no-notice spells as an extra precaution, and Liv had found a self-drive boat-hire place. We would've caught a water taxi, but we didn't want anyone tying us to the scene, and we'd have to drop our no-notice spells to get onboard. The hire place was shut when we went, so we did the next best thing—we "borrowed" one.

Will steadied the small runabout. My hands sweated, and butterflies flew rampant in my belly. There was a foot drop from the wharf into the boat. What if I overbalanced the boat, and we tipped in?

"Come on, Lily. We haven't got all night."

"Can you do a spell to steady the boat?"

He shook his head. "No."

Grrr. I supposed the force of the water pushing against it, making it rock, would take a lot of power to quell. Damn it. He couldn't give me his hand because he was holding the dock so the boat didn't float away since he'd already untied it. I stared at the ebony sky and took a deep breath. Here went nothing. I tried to step down but had to do a little jump because the boat was so much lower than the dock. I landed with a thud, and the boat wavered underneath us, pitching me forward towards the water.

Crap.

My hands shot out in front of me. Will grabbed the back of my T-shirt. I jerked backwards, and as I hit him, he fell onto the bench seat, his arms snaking around me, securing me safely on his lap. He laughed. "I should've known you'd almost fall in. You owe me one."

"Well, if it wouldn't have used so much power to keep the boat steady, I would've done it myself."

"Huh?"

"I figured that's why you refused to do it."

He smirked. "I could have, but I chose not to."

My mouth dropped open. "You did it on purpose, hoping I'd go flying?" Anger funnelled up from the depths of my body. I didn't know whether to punch him or bide my time and push him in later.

"Something like that. Also, remember when I said when you least expect it to expect it?"

"This is payback for the anchovies?"

"Yep. Be thankful I didn't let you fall in. I really, really hate anchovies."

I narrowed my eyes. "Big baby." I slid off his lap and carefully sat next to him. He chuckled as we drifted away from the wharf; then he started the outboard motor. I cringed at the noise and stared back at the building next to the wharf. Hopefully no one was watching, ready to come after us. After we'd made it another minute with no movement on the shore, I sucked in a deep breath. So far so good. But I'd have to give the universe a chance to stuff us up. Sigh.

As we motored across the lagoon, salty air whipped past my face, cooling me down. The distinct odour of Venice—briny with a generous dollop of sewerage—was unmistakable. We didn't say much on the way. Will's jaw was set as he steered in the dark—there were buoy markers to navigate by, but it wasn't like he did this every day. I ruminated over what we should do next if both the factory and Lorenzo's apartment turned up nothing. I chewed my nail, and my leg bounced up and down. *Gah, stop thinking.* I was pretty sure my death grip on the seat was going to give me hand cramps. I needed to relax and not use all my energy before we even got there.

Finally we reached Murano. He pulled in at the same wharf we'd been on yesterday. Was it only yesterday? It felt as if we'd been looking for Angelica for weeks. Time… the construct that was always against us—if we needed it to slow down, it went faster, and during the times we wished it would go faster, it slowed down. Totally disagreeable if you asked me.

Will tied the boat up and stepped out, giving me a hand up onto the wharf. At least we'd done it sans drama this time. I checked my no-notice was still activated. The path was void of anyone else, but nerves still churned my stomach. Lights shone from buildings where people probably lived, and it looked as if there was a small restaurant on the other side of the narrow canal. Fingers crossed no one lived above any of the factories near Lorenzo's place.

Will wasted no time and hurried towards the factory. I had to jog to keep up. He made a BOS. "Once we're there, I'll disable the alarm and cameras. Until I give you the nod, you need to stand guard outside and keep facing away from the wall. We don't want our faces on camera. I'll chuck on a balaclava before I go in."

"Okay." My scalp itched—from the humidity or fear, I didn't know. I wasn't going to argue with anything right now. I just wanted to get in and out.

We reached the factory wall. I made sure I stayed a few metres from it and turned my back. As Will broke in, I slid my phone from my pocket and brought up the camera app—better I was occupied than freaking out. If I didn't keep myself together, I'd be in a foetal position on the ground in no time. *Come on, Lily. You've been in way more dangerous situations. Worst comes to worst, you magic back to the hotel reception room or home.* Surprisingly, that thought took the edge off my fear. No one was about to kill us…. But then again, they'd managed to take Angelica by surprise. Gah!

Once the camera app was ready, I kept an eye on the path and my ears strained. I couldn't look for people coming the other way because then my face would be visible to the camera. I bit my fingernail. How long was Will going to take? I checked my phone again. A minute had passed. At least no alarm had gone off.

A seagull cawed loudly in the distance, and I jumped. Seriously? I tried to slow my sawing breaths. I so wasn't cut out for this kind of stuff. Give me a face-off any day compared to sneaking around.

Tick, tick, tick. Bite, bite, bite. At this rate, I'd have no fingernails left by the time we got back on the boat.

Two minutes.

A hand landed gently on my shoulder. I slammed my hand over my mouth and tried not to scream.

"Hey, it's just me."

I spun around. "I know that… I mean, I figured once I'd survived another shock. Sneaking up on me isn't the answer to all life's problems, you know."

He chuckled. "I didn't think it was."

"You scare me enough that I'm beginning to wonder. You know what I'm like."

"Lily squirrel—yes, I know. Anyway, cameras are disabled. Let's go."

I hurried in after him and shut the door. The showroom door was already open, thanks to Will. We slipped in. I got straight to work and called up my magic. "Show me the last time Angelica was here."

Light filled the space, and I flinched, looking away from my phone screen and checking out behind me. It was dark in real time. *Doh, Lily. What is wrong with you tonight?* I took a few deep breaths and looked at the screen again. Angelica stood with my mother. They were looking at a glass bird. "The last time she was in this room was when we all were."

"Okay. Let's try the factory."

I followed Will in and asked my magic the same question. Again, it showed Angelica standing near the bleachers talking to Lorenzo on the day we'd come to watch him. After that, Will led me to a storeroom where I got nothing, then to two offices…. Again, she hadn't been there at all. This was a bust. Hmm. Maybe if I tried something else. "Show me Lorenzo and Mrs Dal Lago last time they were here."

I blushed. Yikes. It was dark except for the lamp sitting on the desk. They were naked and going for it on that desk. She was under him, and that's all anyone needed to know. I took a photo, which I didn't want to do. Now there was porn on my phone. Porn that wasn't okayed by the perpetrators. When did I turn into a creep?

I showed Will while my gaze looked anywhere but at him and the photo. La, la, la, la, la. Awkward. Well, not as awkward as if my mother were here. At least it was just Will. "Can you take another look and see if that calendar over there is set to a recent date?"

"Okay." I called up my magic and asked to see that again. I stepped around the figures who weren't really there and zeroed in on the desk calendar. I took a photo. "Wow, no wonder his alibi didn't check out. He was here having sex with Mrs D the night Mr D went missing. But why wouldn't they just say?"

Will looked at the photo, then at me. "Because it would be too convenient and make them both look guiltier. At least if his family alibi checked out, it would make him safe. Who wouldn't assume they'd murdered him together knowing what we know now?"

"Hmm, good point."

"If we can figure out what time this was, it'll help. I know she finished work at the hotel at 7:00 p.m.—we have video footage of her in the hotel before that time. Think you can get your magic to work out a time?"

I scrunched my forehead. "I have no idea. It usually does what I say, but I've never been so specific about time before, but I don't see why it wouldn't." I lifted my phone. "Show me this room two nights ago between seven thirty and eight at night." Faded light came in the window, but that was it. Empty. "Show me this room two nights ago between eight and eight thirty." Still Empty. "Show me this room two nights ago between eight thirty and nine." There they were, on the table. "Okay, we have them here between eight thirty and nine, but not before. At least, not in this room. Hang on." I asked for a nine to nine thirty timeline. They were still there, just in a different position. Oh my God. Were you kidding me? Maybe he took Viagra? He had to be at least in his late fifties. I snapped a shot.

Will looked at it. "So the office chair got a workout too?"

"Looks like. It's probably not safe to touch anything in here." I pulled an "ew" face. "I'm thinking we check the other rooms for their presence before that time. See if they were here by themselves earlier or later."

"Good idea."

I held my phone up one last time and asked for nine thirty to ten. She was now resting her bottom on the windowsill smoking a cigarette. He was standing there staring at her. Looked like things were winding down. Finally, ten to ten thirty, they were gone. Thank God. Now it was time to go room to room and see what else was happening here that night.

In the lunchroom, I found where they'd been from seven thirty to eight thirty; they were in here eating dinner, just the two of them, a candle on the table. How romantic. I clicked off a shot. "So, the only time we can't account for is from seven to seven thirty, when I suppose she was showering and getting ready for the date because she's not wearing her work clothes here." Unless work clothes were a tight-fitting red-sequinned dress that finished at the top of her thighs and red stilettos.

"And after ten, we have nothing on them. The crime happened, well became obvious at eleven twenty. So, we have an hour and twenty minutes unaccounted for. As complicated as that spell is, I'm thinking that's enough time to create that kind of masterpiece."

"I guess we have to see if Lorenzo was in his apartment after ten."

"Which will have to wait until tomorrow."

I threw my head back and closed my eyes. And where was Angelica? We'd made some discoveries, but it wasn't enough. Will's arms slid around me, and he pulled me to his chest. "It'll be okay, Lily."

I didn't want to be a naysayer, but…. "It might not be."

He kissed the top of my head. "I know, but we have to have faith that we'll figure this out before whoever did this kills her."

"If it's not those two—and it still could be, but most of their night was accounted for—who would it be? And where does that other dead woman come into it?"

Will swore. "Bloody Agent Tondato. He's making this as difficult as possible. He told me there is no connection to anyone that he can find with that woman and our suspects. I have to trust he's telling the truth, but for all I know, he's made no enquiries."

"But why would he do that?"

"This afternoon, I learnt that they're working on another huge case with the Rome office. It's a dangerous case against the mafia, and they're short-staffed. The horrible truth is that this crime and Angelica's predicament are being shoved to the side."

I looked up at him. "So they're not usually this bad?"

"No. I don't think so, which is both a relief and not a relief. I just wish they would let us take over. At least then I'd have full access to any files they've started and permission to look into more personal things about our victims." He gave me a quick kiss on the mouth. "Let's go. We have something, which is better than nothing, and we'll start fresh tomorrow morning.

I'll call Tondato tomorrow, see if I can wrangle more permissions, and we'll sneak into Lorenzo's apartment. It could be the breakthrough we need."

"Okay. At least we have a plan, but I don't know how much sleeping I'll be doing tonight." Not knowing where Angelica was or what condition she was in, well, it wasn't pleasant. If I did manage to fall asleep tonight, I'd probably have nightmares. Oh, the joy.

We locked up and left, Will reinstating the security cameras and alarm. He set the spell when we were inside but made it so it didn't come into effect for sixty seconds. After the front door was locked, I ran to the front gate and out. He strolled, Mr Nerves of Steel. Crazy man.

As the motor droned and we neared Saint Mark's Square, I took in the lights shining from so many windows. Was Angelica in one of those houses? Was she even still in Venice? Bloody hell. We could look forever and never find her. Dealing with witches was scary times one hundred. Damn it! *Think, Lily.*

I had to raise my voice to be heard above the outboard. "Maybe we should just go and see Lorenzo now and insist on going into his apartment."

"We can't just barge in. Besides, Tondato and his guys checked it out before and found nothing. If we're going to have another crack at this, it has to be under the radar."

"Yes, but they don't have my skills."

"I know that, Lily, but I don't want a call from head office telling us to cease and desist. You know how much Chad hates Angelica. He might threaten firing us again if we keep looking for her."

I sneered. "That's insane. God, I hate that witch." I let out a low scream of frustration.

Will's eyes held understanding. "I know, Lily. I know."

It didn't take much longer, and Will was tying up the boat where we'd found it, and we were climbing out. He grabbed my hand, and we walked back to the hotel holding hands. Imagine taking a walk hand in hand with the man of your dreams through quiet Venetian streets but the romanticism being ruined by the fact that someone you loved was missing, possibly dead. Despair caught in my throat, and I swallowed my tears. I squeezed Will's hand. "I love you."

He smiled. "I love you too."

We were both alert as we neared the hotel, and I opened myself to magic, just in case. My return to sender was up, and my other sight told me Will's was too. My gaze pinged from window to window—both the hotel's and nearby buildings'. Some lights were still on, and music and laughter came from a restaurant on the other side of the square.

It wasn't as late as when Angelica had come home—there'd been no one around then.

We went into the hotel without incident, which I was calling a win. The reception desk was closed for the night, but there was music filtering down the hallway from the bar area.

I shrugged. I was tired because of the stress of the last couple of days, but after our mission, nervous energy had me wide awake. "Why don't we see if anyone's in the bar?" By anyone, I meant our friends. There was probably someone in there, but whether or not they wanted to have a drink with us was another matter.

"Not really. Sorry. I want to go and call James, update him on what we're up to. I might get him to look up some stuff on the system. If it ends up getting back to Chad, then so be it. We need to join some dots before tomorrow if we can." He rubbed the back of his neck. "I have a bad feeling about this." His forehead wrinkles were as deep as ever as he stared at me.

I put my arms around him. "I know. I don't like this either. And the longer this takes…." I didn't need to finish what I was saying.

"It's that and the fact that we're missing something." He made a bubble of silence. "Our two most-likely suspects… there's reasonable doubt as to whether it was them. And if not, we are so far from the truth of all this as we can be. I've never worked on a case we couldn't solve, but this one's getting away from us. And so much is at stake."

I tilted my face up, and he kissed me. If only I had the answers to help and make everything better. But I didn't. Worst feeling ever. "Okay, well, you go upstairs. If anyone's down here, I'll be half an hour. Is that all right?"

He gave me a small smile. "Of course it is. I'll be waiting for you." He waggled his brows, and I chuckled. He gave me a last quick kiss, then turned and started up the stairs. I made my way to the bar hoping Liv or Imani were enjoying a beverage.

There were three groups scattered around—one of four people, one couple, and a large group of ten. But none of them were my friends. I sighed. I wasn't desperate enough to have a drink by myself. Maybe I should text Liv or Imani and ask them to come join me.

I slid my phone out of my pocket, but before I could text anyone, a voice came from behind me. "Hello, Lily."

I spun around. Isabella stood there, dark circles under her eyes but a smile on her face. A few errant hairs stuck out from her plait. I smiled. "Are you going to have a drink?"

"I don't know. I was thinking maybe one vino." She shook her head. "But I'm tired. Would you like to have a quiet drink with me in the restaurant? Everyone has gone home for the night, so it will just be us."

I took one look around the bar and decided it was noisy anyway, and who wanted to yell over the noise to be heard. "Okay. That sounds lovely."

She smiled. "Maybe you try one of my desserts. Tiramisu. I made fresh this afternoon."

"Oh, that sounds lovely. Thank you! But I must pay. This is your business."

She threw her hands in the air. "No! This is my treat. You can help by recommending our 'otel to your friends."

"Okay, then. It's a deal."

I followed her into the hallway and then into the dining room. The muffled quiet was rather soothing. The tables were already set for tomorrow's breakfast, the buffet table clear and awaiting food. Isabella motioned me to a table near the kitchen. Her magic tickled my scalp, and a cake appeared on the table, as did two glasses of a dark red liquid. I sat and lifted a glass to my nose. "Is this a sweet wine?"

"Sì. From Umbria."

I wasn't much of a wine drinker. I'd have a glass some-times, but I was just as happy to have a cocktail…. Okay, I would much rather have a cocktail, but dessert wine was the best of all the wines. "That cake looks delicious! You're an incredible cook."

She pulled her chair out and stood in front of it, placing her hands on the table to help lower herself into the chair. I would've offered to help, but I figured she wanted to do it herself, and if she needed it, she would've asked. I didn't want to offend her or suggest she couldn't do things for herself. She magicked a knife into her hand and cut the cake.

Just as she cut two slices, Francesco walked in through the

main doors. "*Nonna!*" He said something else in Italian, but nonna was the only word I understood. It meant grandmother. They were related? I did my best impression of a poker face, which was more jump the other way than stay neutral. I smiled and pretended the fact that he must be Mr and Mrs Dal Lago's son didn't shock me. He could be a wealth of information if I did this right.

He came to the table and bent to kiss her cheek. She squeezed his cheek and smiled, love clear in her eyes. She looked at me. "This is one of our guests, Lily. Lily, this is my grandson, Francesco."

He gave me a shy smile. "Ciao."

I returned it, although mine wasn't shy. "Ciao. Please, sit with us and have some cake. Your grandmother is a wonderful cook." Isabella gave me a grateful look, although what else would I do? He's her family, and she's sharing free food with me. The least I could do is let her grandson have some. Plus, I wanted information. Maybe this would provide the break we needed... a small clue that would give us a direction.

"Thank you." He walked around his grandmother's chair and sat. "Are you and your friends enjoying your stay?"

Did he get the memo that Angelica was missing? Or did he know something, and he was as good at acting as I was? Whatever it was, it gave me a segue into what I wanted to talk about. "Sort of. The hotel is beautiful, and I love Venice, but my friend is missing—Angelica."

I studied his face, hoping it would give something away. He was around here all the time. Maybe he'd seen something? Or maybe his mother confided in him, if it had been her in the first place. His brow wrinkled, and he pressed his lips together. That told me nothing.

Isabella magicked cake onto our plates. "*Mangia*, mangia."

I didn't know what she said, but context had me guessing. "Eat?"

"Yes. Very good, Lily. Eat, please."

The first mouthful of cake had me stifling a groan of pleasure. This was the best tiramisu I'd ever had. So good. "This is the best, Isabella. Any chance I can come visit in the future and pick up a cake?"

Francesco looked at me. "You mean a piece of cake?"

I grinned. "No, a whole cake."

Isabella chuckled. "Grazie. I would love to cook for you again. You are welcome any time."

As we ate, Francesco stole glances at me, his face serious, almost to the point where I wasn't sure if he was also angry. What had I done? Wanting a whole cake wasn't offensive over here, was it? Maybe he was just upset because his father had been killed. Of course he was. How was I so dumb yet I managed to get to the ripe old age of twenty-five? I'd obviously reminded him that his dad was missing, and his mum was being investigated.

I gave him a sympathetic look. "I'm sorry about your dad."

His eyes watered, and he blinked. Before he could answer, Isabella interrupted. "It is very sad, no? My daughter... she is very upset, and my grandson…. It's 'orrible." Francesco stared at his plate, briefly narrowing his eyes and gritting his teeth. What was that all about? Isabella patted his hand, and he snatched it away. She said something in Italian to him, then turned to me. "We just want to find who did it. It was not my daughter. She would never do anything like that. She loved him." Francesco shook his head ever so slightly, and he pressed his lips together as if he wanted to say something.

There was no way I was going to bring up her infidelities, but maybe her son knew, which was why he was holding back right now. Was it something everyone in the family ignored? Maybe Francesco was sick of it and her behaviour. If he knew it hurt his father, no wonder he was angry. Add to that his grandmother defending Mrs Dal Lago, and, well…. I almost choked on my cake, and I coughed.

Isabella slapped my back a couple of times. She was surprisingly strong for an old lady. "Are you all right?"

I nodded and took a sip of wine to wash the cake down. "I think so. It just went down the wrong way. I'm so clumsy, even when I'm eating."

She stared into my eyes. "Are you sure you're okay?"

I smiled. "Yes. Definitely." *Except that I think your grandson killed his father.* But why did I think that? He wasn't the one doing things wrong. Maybe he hated that his father didn't stand up to his wife or leave her? I mean, if you were going to kill someone, why wouldn't it be her? Or maybe Francesco didn't kill him. Maybe he knew his mum did and was angry that she'd done it? If I were any more confused, I'd be having head spins. Maybe Isabella had forbidden him to say anything? Were they all accessories?

The only way to find out was to keep pushing. Guilt washed through me, and I hated myself, but I'd do anything to find Angelica. Upsetting grieving people was not on my list of things I wanted to achieve, but sometimes we had to do what we hated to get results. Life could be so unfair.

I took a deep breath and looked across the table at Francesco. But before I could say anything, he spoke. "Are you one of those agents?"

"No. I just help them sometimes."

"Your friend who went missing, she's one?"

Time to go fishing. "Yes. We think whoever killed your father has taken her."

Isabella shifted in her seat and glanced quickly at her grandson. He stared at my plate. Was he feeling too guilty to look in my eyes? My leg bounced under the table. He finally looked back up at me. "Do you have any idea who it could be?"

I wasn't going to say anything about Lorenzo—let them think Mrs Dal Lago was the only one left on our radar. "Just your mother. I'm sorry." My heart raced—lying was awful, but I was about to tell a biggie. I needed some kind of reaction… admission… if there was any to give. "I hear they have some new evidence and might be close to making an arrest. I'm so sorry."

His eyes widened, and he turned to his grandmother. She tilted her head to the side and put both hands on one of his. "Bello." Whatever she said next was all in Italian, and I couldn't understand. I subtly took my phone out of my pocket and put it on my lap, drew on my magic, and asked my phone to record. Isabella jerked her head towards me. "Why you use magic?"

"I spilled some wine on my top." I gave her a nervous smile. Crap. The last thing I wanted to do was upset her when so much was going on. What I'd just said wasn't really meant for her, but when else was I going to get an opportunity to speak to him?

Francesco looked at me. "She didn't do it. I know she didn't." He lifted his chin and gave his grandmother a "don't stop me" look. My heart raced. Was he about to confess? She grabbed his forearm, but he shook her off and swung his gaze back to me. Resignation shone from his eyes. I leaned forward. *Please be the breakthrough we're waiting for.*

Isabella's magic tingled my scalp. Was she going to stop him from talking?

Out of the corner of my eye, a dark shape flashed towards me. Before I had a chance to look, something smashed into the side of my head and pain engulfed me. As my head snapped to the right, the last thought before I lost consciousness was that I wasn't going to hear what he had to say.

Damn.

CHAPTER 9

Reluctant awareness. Throbbing head. Nausea, a building eruption swelling through my stomach, my throat. I opened my eyes to pitch-black, sat up slightly, and threw up. And then, because my hands were stuck together, I overbalanced and fell off what must be a bed. The distance to the floor was short but painful. "Oomph." I'd landed on my forearms and front.

Oh, God, what the hell was going on, and where was I?

I tried to pull my arms apart. Not happening. I brought my hands to my face and felt around with my lips. Rope tied my wrists together. I tried to move my feet apart, but they were tied together as well. And just to add to the pain lancing through my head, I'd landed in my own vomit. Had I died and gone to hell? I tentatively felt the left side of my head. An ostrich egg and roughness matting my hair—likely dried blood. No wonder I felt like my head had been smashed in… because it had. Lucky me.

I breathed in and gagged at the vomit odour. Ew. I edged

backwards to escape the worst of the smell. The hard floor was cold but easy to slide on. It was probably terrazzo. Once I was a foot from where I started, I rolled over onto my back and shut my eyes. Where had I been before this? How had I gotten here? Who had hit me, and what had they hit me with?

As I struggled to think, I listened. I was alone—the lack of someone else breathing was a giveaway. Could I still use my magic? There was only one way to find out. I opened myself to the portal. Flickers of magic pulsed through from the river to me. It was less than half of what I was used to, and the flow was sporadic. Still, it should be more than enough to do some simple things.

"Dissolve the ropes around my wrists and ankles." The pressure around my limbs disappeared. I just had to hope whoever had put me here wasn't within sensing-magic distance. I waited for a minute, listening, before I sat up. Sitting up was a terrible idea. Dizziness was like a punch to my face and guts. I carefully lay back down and took some deep breaths. It was me versus my concussion.

After a few minutes, I decided to clean myself up. I didn't move from where I was, but I drew some magic. Unfortunately, not much came through. I waited a bit longer and drew some more. Would my spell work, though? I didn't have a visual on where I was, and the small amounts of power coming through the portal might not be enough to send something to another place. Plus, transporting things was only possible if I could visualise where I wanted it to go. Memories of before here surfaced.

Crap.

Isabella had hit me with something. Was it because her grandson was about to confess that he killed his dad? How long had I been here? It could've been minutes or days. Did Will know I was missing? Hmm, that gave me an idea.

I started to draw on my power, which made me feel worse. Pushing through the pain and vertigo, I visualised all the vomit —what was on the ground and on me, moving to the floor in our hotel room. Gross, I knew, but Will would eventually discover it and know that I was alive. I could've transported it to somewhere else in the hotel, but if Isabella found it, she might suspect it was me and come to finish the job... the job of killing me, not the job of cleaning up.

Before drawing enough power to cast the spell, I blinked and held my breath. Maybe Angelica was here in another room? Was I in an apartment or house?

There was only one way to find out.

I slowly sat up. My head spun, but not as badly as before. I swallowed the urge to vomit. *Okay, so far so good.* Well, sort of. No matter how I spun it, being clobbered in the side of the head and kidnapped wasn't good. But it was an opportunity to find Angelica.

I drew my magic again, which sputtered in and out. It was as if the flow from the river of magic was being held back, then allowed to come through. Could I spell my vomit away reliably, or might it end up halfway to where I intended, unceremoniously dropping from thin air onto an innocent person eating breakfast? Or was it lunchtime? There was no way to tell. *Gah, stop thinking! Just get rid of it.*

I kept drawing magic, filling my natural reserves. Sweat slicked my forehead, and my cheeks heated. I might be overdoing it. Time to let the link to the river go and hope it was enough. "Send all the vomit in this room and on me to the hotel room I slept in the night we came to Venice." That should cover it. I had no idea what day or night it was. What if

I'd lain here for two nights? I shuddered at the prospect. The need to retch overcame me, but I jammed my mouth shut and swallowed. Using magic wasn't the wisest thing with a concussion.

Had it worked? I sniffed. The smell was gone. I patted myself down. Dry! Victory! Time to keep going. Estimating from what had transpired when I awoke, I figured the bed was to my left. Getting on hands and knees, I faced the opposite direction of the bed and carefully crawled until I came to a wall. Once I did that, I followed the wall to the right. It was a massive guess, but if it didn't work out, I'd just go back the other way. The only reason I'd panic is if I was in a doorless, windowless room. I supposed it was possible where witches were concerned. I would make a doorway and leave, but the intermittent power made it sketchy. Maybe I'd try once I'd checked out the room; plus, I needed to look for Angelica, and if I left here, I'd never find my way back.

So, no making a doorway until I'd scoped out the whole place.

I'd reached the end of the wall. I slid my fingers along the adjoining wall, and there it was… a door. Slowly, I stood. My head pounded, but the dizziness was gone. Nausea remained. Unfortunately, there was nothing to be done about my concussion now. If only Beren were here. Ooh, my phone. Oh. My shoulders dropped as I pressed my palms against the door. My phone had been recording on my lap when I was hit. It would still be at the hotel, likely picked up by Isabella or her grandson. Damn!

I took a moment to breathe and focus, then slid my hand down to find the handle. Yay, it turned! I cringed as I opened the door. Would it or would it not squeak? When it was open just enough, I slid through, avoiding any noise. So far so good.

A narrow, horizontal window overlooking a staircase to my left faintly illuminated the hallway. It was night-time, but whether it was midnight or four in the morning, I couldn't tell. Flashing green and red lights intermittently blinked slowly in the blackness. This place must be on the water, so likely I was still in Venice, and from the staircase and lack of a lock on the door, I was on the top floor of a big house rather than an apartment.

Before going down the stairs, it would be prudent to check for Angelica up here first. I threw up a return to sender, in case I came across someone, but as soon as it was in place, it winked out. Damn. That intermittent magic was going to be a problem. I could cast quick spells, but anything that had to stay in place wouldn't work. Was there a weird blip in magic access here, kind of like bad internet reception, or had Francesco and Isabella cast some kind of magic-blocking spell over the house? Whatever it was, it made me more vulnerable.

As a test for later—because as soon as I confirmed whether Angelica was here or not, I wanted to leave—I drew magic from the river. It dribbled through, then stopped, then flowed for a few seconds, then stopped. Grrr. Unlike the internet and modem, there was no way to reset it by turning it off and on again. I stored what I could in my internal magic stash. After a few minutes, I finally had enough to make a doorway, but as soon as I tried to make it, it faded. There wasn't nearly enough time to step through. What would happen if I'd been midway through the door when it disappeared? Would it delete me, drop me in the middle of the lagoon, or cut me in half like I'd done to the love of Dana's life?

Enough of the questions. If I could find Angelica, she'd know.

Then the best idea ever happened. I could try and contact

Will. When that stupid vampire witch had tried to kill me, we'd managed to talk over a long distance. This should be easy. I tried to ignore the thudding ache in my brain and concentrated on Will, on how much I loved him, what he sounded like, what he looked like, what his magic felt like. I drew on my core power. There he was! I could sense him. *Will. Will, it's Lily.*

Lily?! His mind voice sounded frantic and relieved all at the same time. *Wh— r—*

Crap. It was like trying to talk over a line that was breaking up. I growled, then tried again. *Will?*

Nothing. *Damn, damn, damn, damn, damn.* I sighed. I'd have to try again soon. Maybe I'd search the next couple of rooms and have another go. I made my way down the hallway. Another door to my right must be a room that backed onto the bedroom I'd just come from. I placed my ear against the door and listened. Silence. I gripped the handle and turned it super slowly, then pushed the door gently. I could've cried with happiness when no squeaks screamed, "Lily's wandering around!" At least someone had been maintaining this place.

This room was as dark as the last one, although a sliver of moonlight seeped in from the hallway. It was enough to make out shadows, but little else. I couldn't tell if anyone was in here from my position in the doorway. Did I try and cast a trickle of light, or did I walk in and feel around? If someone was asleep in here, surely the faint light wouldn't rouse them? I debated for a few throbs of my head—what I wouldn't give for a headache tablet about now.

I opened the portal of magic and syphoned some through to my personal reservoir. A small light wouldn't take much at all. I held my hand out, palm up. Hopefully this would work without calling the killer witches down on my head. My heart galloped as I said in my mind, *Cast faint light.*

A golf-ball-sized glow hovered in my palm, subtly illuminating the room… the empty room. I took a shuddering breath. The only things in here were a bed, freestanding wardrobe, and a dressing table and chair. I willed the light brighter. There was no evidence of Angelica having been in here recently. On to the next room.

The next room was an empty bedroom, too, and the next —a bathroom through a door at the end of the hall opposite the stairs—was also void of life. There was one more door on this level, then I'd have to try downstairs. What if she wasn't here? *Think about that later if you need to.* My brain was right, but before I tried the next room, I wanted to attempt talking to Will again.

I drew power from my stomach reserves and concentrated. Sharp pain stabbed my forehead. I cringed and shut my eyes tight, but I wouldn't give up. *Will. Will, can you hear me?*

Yes! Where are you?

I have no idea. In a house—

Lily?

Damn. I must be breaking up. Fatigue broke over me as my magic was close to being depleted. I stopped drawing from it and, leaning my back against the wall, slid to the floor. I hung my head and shut my eyes. *Breathe in. Breathe out.* I stayed that way for a few minutes, trying to regain some energy. I opened myself to the river of magic and took in as much as I could in fits and starts. Frustration balled my fists. Searching this house was going to take forever.

Maybe it was time to stop worrying about speaking to Will. There wasn't much else I could tell him… well, except for Isabella and Francesco, but I couldn't tell him where I was. Maybe I should just try walking out the front door when I was done? Whatever spell was on the house wouldn't be outside. Such a genius, not thinking about it before. But to be fair to my brain, I had concussion. All I really wanted to do was lie in the foetal position and sleep for two years. If I did manage to find Angelica, I sure hoped she was in better condition than me; otherwise, how in the hell would I move her? Yet again, a problem for when it came time... if it came time.

I swallowed and laboriously got to my feet. I grabbed the handle on the last upstairs door and slowly pushed down. When the door opened, it didn't make a noise, but a pulse of power pushed me back a step. Then it was gone. I froze and strained my ears. What the hell was that? I glanced back into the hallway and at the stairs. It all looked the same in the gloom.

I wished for my return to sender as I stepped into the room. Before I could chicken out, I created a small light in my palm. As the glow melted into every corner of the room, I sucked in a breath. Angelica! She was asleep or unconscious— I refused to think dead—lying on a single bed against the far wall.

I hurried over and whispered as loudly as I dared. "Angelica. Angelica." The light still hovering over one palm, I reached out with my other hand, my breath coming faster, my heart racing. *Please don't be cold.* My fingertips alighted on her cheek. She was warm. Just to be sure, I felt her neck for a pulse. Oh my God, yes. I hitched in a deep breath of relief. I grabbed her shoulder and shook. "Wake up. Angelica, it's me, Lily."

Crap.

She wasn't responding at all. What had they done to her? I

drew some fitful magic from the river to my reservoir. It was time to try Will again. *Will?*

I'm here.

I found Angelica. She's alive but unconscious.

Where are you?

Were they footsteps echoing from the stairs? I extinguished my light, just in case. *I don't know. Venice somewhere? I think someone's coming.* Yep, definitely footsteps. They stopped down the hallway, probably at the top of the stairs. Crap. I snuck to the door and peered around. A figure stood at the open doorway to the room I'd woken up in. The person was shorter than me, about my build, maybe slightly wider? It didn't look like Francesco—he was too thin and taller than me. His mother was about my height, so it had to be Isabella. Was she here to help me or kill me? *Mmm, dumb question, Lily, since she was the one who clocked you in the head.* There was my answer.

The light went on in my room. Yep, it was definitely Isabella. Had the pulse of power when I'd opened Angelica's door been an alarm of sorts?

I ducked back into Angelica's room and silently shut the door. Surely Isabella would come looking for me in here next. I glanced around for somewhere to hide. There was one freestanding wardrobe, but that was too obvious. Maybe under the bed? I dropped to hands and knees and lifted the sheets that draped beneath the mattress. Yes! There was plenty of space. I crawled in, disturbing dust. Choking, I coughed into my arm. I hoped like hell that she hadn't heard me. Although, for all she knew, it could be Angelica. Still, if I wasn't where I was supposed to be, I was likely here somewhere. I shook my head at my exceptional logic. *Good one, Lily.*

Now to wait. After that, who knew. I couldn't beat her with magic…. Except, what if she couldn't draw magic because of the wards on the house? At this stage, I had to assume that's what was blocking the magic. I'd never come across another situation where access to the river of power behaved like an internet connection, which, let's be honest, wasn't great in Venice in amongst the tightly packed buildings. If I sensed her casting a spell, I'd jump straight on my return to sender, just in case she'd turned the power back on, so to speak. Being a civilian, it was unlikely she'd know what a return to sender was, so I'd have the upper hand.

Footsteps shuffled outside the door. I tried to breathe as quietly as possible, but it sounded as loud as a freight train. It probably didn't, but that's what it felt like. I could just see the bottom of the door. It opened. Isabella's shoes stood there for a moment, then the light switch clicked, throwing light into every corner of the room. Because of the dangling sheet, she wouldn't be able to see me unless she actually got on the floor and looked under the bed. Fingers crossed she was too old to physically do it.

She stepped into the room. Crap. Maybe they really didn't want to hurt us. If they had, wouldn't Angelica be dead already? She wasn't turned to glass as far as I could tell. Maybe they just wanted to slow down the investigation? Although kidnapping and injuring a PIB agent was a sure way to get you thrown in jail when it was all over. So now they had more to lose. It didn't make sense.

Her black orthopaedic sandals brought her all the way to the bed. I cringed at the proximity of her feet to my face. Gross. I could clearly see the cracked skin of her big toe. It was literally within spitting distance. I shuddered. Why me? My gag reflex kicked in. Oh, God, I needed to keep quiet. If she found me because I was dry heaving over the proximity of her feet, I'd be so annoyed. I wanted to look away from the feet, but I needed to know if she found me and was going to do something. There was no option but to suffer.

She said something in Italian—to herself or Angelica, I had no idea. She turned and walked in the direction of the wardrobe. The door creaked open, and after a moment, the thud of it closing had adrenaline ramping up in my body, increasing my heart rate and making me hyperaware. I itched to jump out of my hiding place and run, but I gritted my teeth and stayed. If the universe was in a good mood, maybe she'd leave without finding me.

The feet came back to the bed. Damn it.

"Lily, are you under there?"

Double damn it. Bloody universe.

"Lily?"

I didn't answer. If she was going to find me, she'd have to work for it.

"You going to make an old woman get on the floor?"

Yes, yes I was. And I wouldn't even feel guilty for it.

Her knees bent, and the mattress squeaked as she rested her hands on it and slowly lowered herself to the floor. Once she knelt, it wasn't long before her eyes peered under the bed, and our gazes met.

The game was up.

She smiled a grandmotherly smile—should I trust it or not? Hmm, she'd smashed me in the head and could've killed me. If I trusted her, I was an even bigger idiot than I gave myself credit for. "Why did you hit me? You could've killed me."

"I know. I'm sorry. I must protect my family. My daughter, she is an idiot. I told her not to marry him, but she didn't listen. The only good thing to come from that marriage was my grandson. Now, get out from there. If I stay here much longer, I will not be able to get up."

Like I cared. Maybe I should push her over and run. But could I really do that to an elderly lady? She wasn't threatening me right now, which made hurting her impossible. Injuring a defenceless-looking person went against everything I stood for. Yes, she'd assaulted me earlier, but if her intent had been to kill me, I'd already be dead. At least, that's what I told myself. "What if I don't want to get up? And what happens now? If you kill me or Angelica, you'll be hunted down by the PIB. You might be trying to save your family, but not only will whoever killed Mr Dal Lago go to jail, you will too for kidnapping me."

She started laughing. Her chuckle quickly billowed to hysterics. She guffawed as tears streamed down her cheeks. What the hell? This was the moment I should've picked to slide out from under the bed and run, but even though she was incapacitated, she blocked the way. I sighed. This was not going to plan. *How unusual.*

Dust tickled my nose, and I sneezed.

"*Salute.*"

I figured that meant bless you. "Grazie." Look at me, being all Italian and stuff.

At least Isabella had stopped laughing. Staying here would solve nothing, so I supposed it was time to get out from under here and reassess the situation. Angelica couldn't save herself, so it was up to me. "All right. I'll come out."

She smiled. "Good girl." Isabella stood and moved out of my way.

I slid out and got to my feet. Dust coated my front. I patted myself down, sending motes into the air, which made me sneeze again. Angelica, however, slept on. My forehead tightened. "What did Francesco do to her?"

Isabella blinked at me and shook her head. "You really are stupid. I like you, but you are not very smart." God, if smashing someone over the head was what she did to people she liked....

"Excuse me?" So much for being a nice old lady. If she kept this up, I *would* push her over.

Angelica groaned. I snapped my head around. Her head lolled to one side, and her eyes moved behind her lids. Isabella's magic tingled my scalp. I looked at her. A needle appeared in her hand. She stepped up to the bed and leaned down to stick it in Angelica's arm.

I grabbed Isabella's arm. "No! I can't let you do that."

She strained against my hold, the needle inching closer to Angelica's arm. "I want her sleeping."

"I don't." My voice came out in a pant. Damn, she was strong. I tried to draw magic. A trickle came through. I willed the needle part of the syringe onto the hallway floor. She'd have no idea where it was, and the closer I tried to send it, the more likely it was to disappear with the way the magic was blinking in and out.

Just as the metal tip pierced her skin, the needle disappeared. I let go of Isabella, and she fell forward onto Angelica. The old lady awkwardly righted herself and turned to face me, her lips pinched with anger. "You don't understand. She doesn't know who put her here. This is for her own safety. If she sees me, I'll have to kill both of you."

My mouth dropped open. And I'd thought she was kind of nice. Was it crazy of me to be just a little hurt? I thought she liked me. "You're going to kill me?"

"Of course. As you said, I hit you and kidnapped you. I don't want to go to jail. Once my family is safe, I will make sure Angelica is returned alive. You shouldn't have asked so many questions. Francesco never listens. It's not his fault though. My daughter never listens either. If she had, none of this would've happened."

"Right, so everything is everyone else's fault?"

She regarded me with a look of complete righteousness. "Of course. I always have to fix everything. Who do you think made the 'otel a success? Who do you think looked after Francesco when Elena was off with one of her men and Antonio drank himself stupid? I am not a young woman anymore. I am tired, and I want to enjoy the years I have left. I've given up more than enough for this family."

"What did you have to give up?" Maybe if she thought I cared, she'd decide not to kill me? Not that I was going to let her. The only problem was my reluctance to hurt her. If she tried to kill me, though, I guessed I'd have to get over myself. I resisted the urge to look at Angelica to see how she was. I hoped she wouldn't groan again and remind Isabella that she needed sedating.

"My brilliant career, not that women are encouraged as artists, but I could've started late. If my grandson hadn't needed me so much... if his father wasn't such an idiot." She blew out a breath and waved her hand around. "When I was young, my paintings were shown in a gallery once, and then I started glass-blowing. Why don't I show you?" Her magic tickled my scalp, and a glass sculpture of a bird appeared in her hand, a pigeon.

I leaned closer to study the detailed work. "You did that?" She looked at me again but said nothing. I slapped my forehead. "Oh, right. *You* killed your son-in-law. But why?" Yay that I'd finally, with more than a lot of hints, figured out who the murderer was, but poo that it took until I was at said murderer's mercy before I did. I was putting it down to the fact that I wasn't the only one on holiday—my brain was right there along with me. I tried to ignore the icy fingers of fear skating down my back.

"He let my daughter have her way with everything. But he would never leave her, no matter how much they fought. It made my life difficult." She pressed her lips together. "I put up with it for many years, but my… how you say… last straw was when he killed the pigeons in the courtyard." She shook her head, anger radiating from her eyes. "He should not have done that."

"I love pigeons… all birds actually." Maybe I should try and turn myself into a pigeon to save myself? At the very least, I needed a bird costume. Should I start cooing? Honestly, after all I'd been through, if I was killed because of a freaking pigeon, I was going to be severely crapped off.

"Are you listening to me?"

"Oh, sorry. I was… thinking about pigeons. They're so cute. I love feeding them, and how cool are they in Saint Mark's Square, landing all over people." Okay, and pooing on them, but I didn't want to get into that now. The longer I kept her talking, the better. I needed more time to find a way out of this.

She smiled. "Yes, they are beautiful creatures. They bring life to the square. They have always been good company too. I once had a pigeon familiar, but he died ten years ago." She sniffed. "I have been sad since he has gone."

"I'm so sorry. That is sad."

She nodded. "Thank you. You are a lovely girl. I'm sorry I have to kill you. I really am." Her magic prickled my scalp, and the pigeon disappeared.

What the hell? I looked at the ceiling and threw my arms in the air. I hated being nice for nothing, well, not for nothing, but when it gets thrown back in your face, like letting people merge into your lane when you're stuck in traffic. They push in by racing down the inside lane knowing people are parked there, and then they don't even do a thank-you wave. Is it wrong that I always wished those people would crash their car? Hmm, being a witch, I *could* make them crash their car, and no one would ever know.... *No, bad Lily.*

Angelica groaned, snapping me out of my reverie. Isabella's magic tickled my scalp, and a new needle materialised in her hand. She pushed my chest, and I stumbled backwards, away from her and Angelica.

"No!"

She stabbed the needle into Angelica's arm. I found my footing and leaped to Isabella, shoving her out of the way—old lady or not, she was crazy and dangerous. The needle stuck out of Angelica's arm, but no fluid had gone in yet. As I ripped it out, Isabella's magic tickled my scalp. Crap. I drew from the river of power, but it was still glitchy—she must have a way around it. Damn it!

The needle disappeared from my grasp and shot into Angelica's arm. For God's sake. This was getting ridiculous. I moved to grab it again, but Isabella's power slammed into me. It was as if a strong wind buffeted me, pushing me backwards. I tried to brace against it, lean forward. Just a few inches and I'd be able to touch the needle.

I strained my muscles and grunted with the effort. *Come on. Just a couple more inches.* The plunger slid down, pushing the liquid into Angelica's body. "Nooooooo!"

And then it was done.

The wind died, and I flew forward, only saving myself by

falling on top of Angelica. Annoyance gave way to seething anger, which heated my insides almost as much as drawing too much magic. Even if she wasn't trying to kill Angelica, she could end up overdoing it by accident, not to mention, I was hoping Angelica would be able to help us escape. She might know the spell that was cutting off our magic and be able to undo it or something.

Isabella gave me a "you shouldn't have done that" look and drew more magic. I tried to draw consistent power to make a return to sender. I just managed to get it up when her spell hit, but then my protection failed as the magic winked out again. She must have cast a freeze spell because she stood there, not moving, and my limbs felt heavy, like I couldn't take more than one or two steps even if I wanted to. Hopefully, I managed to deflect more of the spell than I got. I turned with the speed of a teenager who'd just been told to hurry up and get ready for school. Hoping Angelica would be safe because she posed no threat, I tried to move towards the door.

Did I have gravity boots on? Trying to lift my foot off the floor was worse than walking through knee-deep mud. Even my breathing had slowed. Sweat popped out on my forehead as my right foot came completely off the floor, moved forward in slow motion, and landed. Time for my left foot. I couldn't turn my head quickly either, so I was still half looking at Isabella and half at the door. She hadn't moved. Did that mean she couldn't draw power to undo the effects of the spell or was that even impossible with power after the fact? If only I had more of an idea of how all this worked. Whatever it was, I was winning because I could move and she couldn't.

My left foot inched through the air and dropped to the ground, my leg more bent than normal. Looked like gravity was going to help me get the job done. All I had to do was get my foot up and forward. It would make for some noisy tread-ing, but I didn't need to sneak anymore. The only risk was if I fell. Oh, God. How the hell would I get back up again? It would take an hour, which was pretty depressing for someone who was sober or someone who hadn't just broken both legs and an arm. Note to self: don't put your foot too far forward, and keep the leg bent.

I managed two more steps. I hadn't turned my head all the way forward because I wanted to keep an eye on Isabella. It was a good thing I had—she was lifting a foot even more slowly than I was. I had the upper hand, although this was ridiculous. The slowest chase in history.

After a couple of minutes, I was halfway to the door and exhausted. Sheesh. This was akin to smashing out weights at the gym. The subtle scrape of Isabella's magic scored the back of my neck. Crap. Now what? If she was able to reverse the spell on herself, I was in major trouble.

Her smile was more catlike than pigeonish. She shook her arms and legs, as if testing them. "Ah, *bene.*"

Ah, not bene. I knew that meant good. It was so not.

I let my foot drop to the floor. A snail could catch me at the rate I was moving. Instead, I'd just have to keep trying to draw power and hope I could suck in enough to keep her at bay. There must be some reason she hadn't killed me yet, since that's what she'd decided had to happen. Hmm, if she'd been turning people into glass sculptures and it needed a lot of power, maybe she'd worn herself out and was still recovering? I knew how that felt, straining yourself to the absolute limit. It'd landed me in bed for days at a time, and I was young. I narrowed my eyes. It was a slow and embarrassing manoeuvre. That's why she must've been cooking the non-witch way! She didn't have the energy to magic the food. It all made sense.

Maybe I had a chance after all.

She moved and stood between me and the door. "You need not try to run. I have locked this house with magic. You can never escape." She cocked her head to the side, studying me. Nodding, she folded her arms. "I will make you into a masterpiece!" She grinned. "You will be my best work. Instead of putting you outside where they will take you away, I can move you to an art gallery, and people will marvel over your beauty." She nodded. "Si, perfetta. I did not get the credit I deserved for Antonio or Violetta, even though I saw those people amazed at the beauty of my work. I will make a new name so they will not know who I really am. Then I can enjoy my success."

Oh crap. Isabella was ten types of crazy. This was a new and even worse way to be objectified. Was she going to undress me first? When I tried to talk, my lips and tongue were heavy, reluctant. My words came out in a drunk-on-a-bender slur— which was much worse than the usual drunken slur. It would be a surprise if she could understand me. "A... togaaa... wooould... beee... nicccccce." If I was going to be immortalised, she could at least let me pick what to wear, and since I was in Italy, a toga would make things feel more classical. Also, I did not want to be naked in public for eternity.

"Silly girl. I cannot understand you." She cupped my cheek with her hand. "Ah, such youthful skin. Much easier to work with than Violetta and Antonio." My mouth would've dropped open, but nothing was happening quickly, except for my thoughts because who wouldn't want to be lucid when they were about to die? And, yes, that was totally sarcastic. I always hoped when I died that it would come as a total surprise for one hundredth of a second or even when I wasn't looking. I did not want to know ahead of time.

We didn't always get what we wished for, obviously.

She ran a hand over my head. "Your hair will turn out well. Yes. Much better than your friend's." She turned her head to glance at Angelica before looking back at me. My eyes widened, albeit slowly, and Isabella grinned. "Ah, you thought I was telling the truth before? I lied. She found my button." Her magic tingled my scalp, and the pearlescent blue button in the photo I'd taken of Angelica sat in her palm. "Of course I'm going to turn her into a sculpture as well. Maybe we show you together at the gallery? I didn't want you to have extra… how you say… incentive to stop me before." She magicked the button away.

The spell I was under didn't prevent my stomach from dropping like a rollercoaster car. What would losing both of us do to my mum, and everyone else? The pressure of frustration built inside me until I thought I'd explode. This couldn't be happening. I needed to think about something else otherwise my brain would stay on a panicked loop.

I knew why she was going to kill us, but I wanted to ask why she'd killed that old lady—Violetta. Where did she fit into it? The only thing worse than dying? Dying without knowing the answer to a puzzle. It was all I had to cling to right now, so I was taking it.

I opened myself to the power and sucked in little by little, moving it to my internal reserves. It might take a while, but if I had enough time, I'd end up with a sufficient amount to do something to Isabella. I just wasn't sure what. And if I did kill her, would her protection spells on the house disappear, or would Angelica and I starve to death? *Argh! Don't worry about that. You'll find a way—you always do.* My heart wanted to race, but the half-strength freeze spell wouldn't let it.

Isabella clicked her fingers in front of my face. "Lily? Lily, you are not listening to me. This is very rude of you." I would've shrugged, but by the time it happened, she'd be onto the next thing. Instead of doing or slurring anything, I syphoned more power across. "I do not like to work in this space. I will move you to my studio."

Damn it! What if her studio was in a different building? There would be no way to find Angelica later. Hmm, unless I could do something to the outside of the building that basically said "Angelica and Lily are here." But what?

Before I had time to figure it out, she'd made a doorway around me. The room disappeared, and a different one materialised. It looked to be a reception room with the same terrazzo floor as the room I'd just been in. Were we still in the same house?

The door opened, and Isabella stood behind a wheelchair. She pushed it into the room and shoved me into it. "There. Much easier. Let's get you into my studio." I wanted to scream, but it would achieve nothing but tiring me out. Frustration sizzled beneath my skin. How dare she just manhandle me like that, treat me like I was an inanimate object to be moved about at her whim. It was as if she no longer saw me as a person. I'd become her next project. Possibly, in her mind, I was already made of glass—no longer alive, devoid of feelings.

But I wasn't, dammit!

She pushed me down a hallway and into a large room that again had all windows covered. Even if I had been able to see out, it was still night-time, the landscape shrouded in darkness. It wouldn't have helped me much, if at all.

An easel stood in the middle of one wall, and paintings hung from every available surface—Venetian landscapes and still lifes. A rustic green industrial-looking cabinet with small drawers stood about chest height, its top covered with all manner of small-animal glass sculptures. Oh my God, was that someone's cat in amongst the pigeons, sparrows, mice, and fish? Hopefully, it had been an old cat ready to die before she did that to it.

She moved me to the middle of the room and used magic to lift me out of the chair. She manually adjusted my legs so they were straight rather than bent, and then I was standing. "Oh, splendido!" She grabbed my left wrist and used her other hand in an attempt to bend my elbow. Stuff making it easy for her. Even though I couldn't move, I could still tense my muscles, making my arm rigid and unyielding. That's right— there would be no more yielding today. All yielding was over, finished. I was not a mannequin. If I had my way, I'd make sure I was the worst-posed sculpture ever. If I could foil her attempts at a visually pleasing pose, maybe I'd be too ugly to ever display. That would suit me just fine.

She released my arm, then slapped it. "Boh!" She said some choice words in Italian whilst waving her arms. I could only assume she was swearing by the tone of her voice and her pinched expression. One point to me, zero to Isabella. I would have fist pumped, but, well, you know.

"Stop making this difficult."

I painstakingly cracked a smile. Luckily, I was still feeling the mood when I finally reached maximum up-curl. Was that what it was like to be a tortoise or a sloth? By the time you could reveal your emotions on your face, the feeling had already passed.

She narrowed her eyes. "I prefer that you are alive when I start this process—the sculpture will be more lifelike. But I can kill you first, and it will still be beautiful."

The warm flood of adrenaline lazily seeped through my belly, making me realise I needed to go to the toilet. Gah, what a time to notice. I pushed the thought away. I was not dying today. No way. I sucked in more power. It was never enough, but it was something to add to what was already there. I needed to concentrate, not get distracted by Isabella, so when she grabbed my wrist again, I let her treat me as if I were a Barbie doll. She arranged my left arm so it was bent, and my hand was on my hip. The other arm, she lifted vertically, with a slight bend in the elbow. My hand was bent back and flat, ready for something to rest on my palm. Her magic scraped the back of my neck, and something heavy, hard, and cold settled in my palm. My arm started bending more with the weight until she put her hand underneath it to stop it falling.

"Hmm." She thought for a moment. Her magic returned, and whatever was on my hand disappeared. I couldn't turn or raise my head fast enough to see what it was. Her eyes lit up, and she nodded, a self-satisfied smile on her face. She drew more magic, and something cool, heavy, slippery, and firmly squishy moulded to my palm, and around the back of my neck. What the hell? *Gah, don't be distracted. Suck in more magic.*

I didn't listen to myself. Instead, I looked down to whatever was hooked around the back of my neck and draping down my front. A gurgling noise came from my throat. Isabella laughed. "Do not worry, Lily. It is just a python."

Just a python?! Snakes weren't my favourite things, but then again, I didn't have a phobia of them—I liked to think of it as a healthy respect. We had so many poisonous snakes in Australia that it was sensible to want to stay away from them, but pythons were harmless… unless you were a small dog, rat, or possum. I was none of those, so I should be okay.

I took a slow, calming breath—I could hardly take any other kind of breath, and at this point, I was happy any breath was going in.

Focus. I opened myself up to the river of power and absorbed more magic. The snake, which had the top part of its body draped over my hand, slid down my arm and to my other shoulder as Isabella stared, apparently mesmerized. I did my best to ignore the sensation of the snake roaming my body. Even at the slow rate I was gathering power, I would soon have enough to do something decent. I needed maybe another twenty minutes or so. Then I could kill her. Hmm, should I kill her though? Was there something I could do to disable her until I could get help, or would I just be dooming myself to a slow death? Surely, even with my sluggish movement, I could escape?

I took in more power.

My arm, which was naturally not going to stay in the air forever, ached. The freeze spell usually defied gravity, but this was only half a freeze spell. I did my best to relax my arm, and it inched down. The snake had also moved towards the floor. It had wrapped once around my body, and its head was at my shin. Maybe wrangling the snake would keep Isabella somewhat occupied. She put her hands on her hips as she observed both of us.

Deeper divots formed within her already-wrinkled forehead. Her magic prickled my scalp, and the snake stopped moving. She crouched awkwardly and gathered as much of it as she could from just below the head, then wrapped it around my neck. The snake dangled there. Had she killed it?

She forced my arm back into its original position and draped the front of the snake over my hand again. "I have stunned it so we have no more problems. I cannot force him to stay there otherwise, so I will sculpt him first. It won't hurt you too much—just where the snake touches your skin."

I blinked in slow motion. What was she talking about? The

snake wasn't just touching my hand, but it was wrapped around my arm, the back of my neck, and trailed down one side of my body, to the inside of one leg, and around the back of the other ankle. It was touching a lot of places. And what kind of pain were we talking about? I shut my eyes. Molten glass would give me third-degree burns. I was pretty sure nothing was more painful than that. And that poor snake. Tears moistened my eyes, but I bit my tongue, refusing to let her see how angry and frustrated I was. She had to be one of the evilest people I'd come across. She was giving Piranha a run for her money.

I refocussed. If I didn't act now, I probably wouldn't get the chance. I doubted I'd be able to concentrate enough on magic if I were burning half to death. But what was I going to do? Did I have enough power for anything permanent? If I only half hurt her, there was no way I could gather enough power in time for a second try, and that was if she didn't kill me on the spot.

I breathed deeply in through my nose and did my best to not panic, to contain the rising dread within me. I couldn't shut down now, or that would be the end of it... the end of me.

Isabella made one last adjustment to the snake and turned my head to look up at the animal draped over my palm. Great, so she was making me watch. I welcomed the anger that built in my belly. How had I ever thought she was grandmotherly and nice? I was such a bad judge of character. And who did she think she was, ruining what was the most well-deserved holiday in the history of holidays. My mother had only just been rescued. This might break her... the last nail in the coffin, so to speak. We'd only just been reunited, something she'd been waiting for, for the last ten years. Seeing James and me again had been what had kept her going. *Damn you, Isabella. You are not destroying my family.*

I syphoned another dribble of magical river, and another. It was like being made to slowly sip through a broken straw when you desperately wanted to gulp down the whole drink.

When Isabella drew more power and started chanting, I knew this was it. It was now or never. But I still wasn't sure what to do. I moved my eyeballs as fast as they would go, searching for a projectile I could possibly send flying across the room to stab her with. I could've set her hair on fire, but that would require immense amounts of magic to build up sufficient heat, and I didn't have enough.

Then I spied the glass ornaments. She was turned side-on to them and wasn't paying attention. There was no way she'd realise what was happening till it was too late. Did I have enough magic to send that cat flying into her skull? I'd like to think the cat would be happy to know it helped get revenge on the person who killed it. *Right, cat. It's you and me. Please don't fall to the floor halfway to my target.*

I sucked in one last blip of power and was about to tell my magic what to do when a door shut towards the front of the house, and a male voice called out, "Nonna! *Dove sei?*" No, no, no, no, no! Francesco was here. Why, out of all the bad timing in the world, did it have to be now? A tear escaped the confines of my eye. *Don't waste this opportunity.* I took in a smidge more power. Maybe he would just say hello and then leave her to do her thing?

He strode through the door, and she turned to look at him, the prickle of her magic subsiding. Francesco saw me and stopped dead. His mouth dropped open. Thank God I wasn't naked yet. He turned his gaze to his grandmother and raised his voice. I had no idea what he was saying.

She rolled her eyes and moved her hands in an intricate conversational dance to punctuate whatever she was saying, possibly imploring him to stop being silly and go away. He shook his head, and she folded her arms. Maybe this wasn't as bad as it seemed? Maybe he'd save me? I turned my gaze on him, hoping he could see how desperate I was for help, but he wasn't looking at me. He was still fixated on his grandmother.

Finally, he threw one hand in the air and looked to the ceiling. He crossed his hands in front of his body and then moved them apart in one quick motion. *"Basta. Ho finito."* He flicked his gaze to me, then dropped his head to look at the ground. I knew, in that moment, that he'd given up.

She made a violent shooing motion, and he turned and walked away, taking my hope with him. I absorbed a trickle more power. I'd just have to wait for him to leave and return to my original plan. I. Was. Not. Giving. Up.

By the time he stepped back through the door, she'd started her chant again, her magic humming uncomfortably along my scalp. I shuddered. All the places the snake touched my skin warmed. Oh, crap. Also, that poor snake. I wasn't sure if it was dead or just asleep. I hated that she was going to burn it alive, encase it in glass. Sorrow swept through me at the thought of her other victims—witches and animals alike.

Should I try and throw that cat, or should I go for something smaller? Surely if I was accurate, a bird could do the job, and I could probably throw it with more force. Damn. This was so risky. I'd stick with the cat.

I tapped into the power in my belly and silently said, *Smash that glass cat into Isabella's temple as hard as you can.* The cat flew across the room, but we were too far from it, and it lost height as it went. By the time it reached her, it thumped into her hip. She staggered sideways and grunted, but it didn't achieve anything except to annoy her before it fell to the ground with a loud clunk. Glass around the tail smashed off, revealing bone underneath. Ew.

Most of my magic reserves were gone, only what I needed to survive left, and if things continued as they were, I wouldn't need those small reserves for long.

Isabella shook her head. "You dare!" she screamed.

Oh, God, here we go. I'd poked the bear rather than killed it.

She drew more power, the air charged with it. A thick layer of tiny glass beads coated the snake. Heat built. Hotter and hotter. Not hot enough to melt the glass, but hot enough to be uncomfortable. The temperature rose. It reached the level I'd snatch my hand away from a flame. Then it increased again. My stomach tightened as searing agony whipped my body.

Even the half-freeze spell wasn't enough to stop me.

I opened my mouth and screamed, the sound echoing off the terrazzo floors and brick walls.

This couldn't be happening. I was out of options. Was there another way I could access the river of magic? There had to be a way around her spell.

The sweetly sick scent of burning flesh tainted the air, and I moved involuntarily, albeit ridiculously slowly, my body doing its best to escape the blistering pain. My arm lowered an inch at a time, but the pain didn't stop. Isabella's face contorted into anger as she stepped towards me, her lips moving with whatever spell she was using to melt the glass.

I didn't see how this could end any other way than with me dead.

Francesco silently ran into the room. Was he coming back to help her finish the job more quickly? He drew power—I remembered how his power felt from when he moved our bags on the first day. His lips moved, but no sound came out.

Isabella's intonating ceased, surprise registering in her eyes. The molten heat stopped increasing. Was it cooling slightly? Not to get me wrong, I was still writhing as much as my limited movement allowed, but it seemed as if the heat was dissipating.

Francesco walked around Isabella until he was between us, facing her. He spoke to her in Italian, his voice rising and falling. I wished I knew what he was saying. If her eyes were any indication, she was livid. He turned to me, at first horror, then sadness in his gaze. His magic tickled my scalp, and the snake disappeared, ripping skin from my shoulder. I screamed again, and tears slid down my cheeks. I needed to pant through the pain, but I couldn't….

But then I could.

The freeze spell disappeared.

I swayed before my knees collapsed. Francesco jumped in front of me, catching me under the arms. "I am so sorry, Lily. Oh, Dio, please forgive me for not helping you earlier."

A wave of relief smashed over me, and I managed to rasp, "Thank you," before the burden of pain was too great, and my awareness decided it had had enough.

As I slid into blackness, I hoped Francesco didn't change his mind.

CHAPTER 10

I awoke to light streaming through the window and the absence of pain. I squinted against the brightness.

"Lily, are you awake?" Hope tinged my mother's worried voice, and relief cascaded through my body.

I opened my eyes further and turned to lie on my back. Mum rose from the chair at the small table and came and sat next to me, the mattress dipping slightly. For some strange reason, we were still in the hotel in Venice. "Yep, I'm awake and blessedly pain-free."

She smiled, her eyes glistening with what I figured were tears. She bent, wrapped her arms around me, and squeezed tightly. "We were beside ourselves with worry when you disappeared. I would've died if we didn't get you back." She sat up and looked down into my eyes. "How are you?"

"Tired."

"Beren healed you at that place. That young man, Francesco, he came and got us. Thank God he's a decent person. His grandmother… what a witch."

"There's stronger language I could use."

"Yes, I'm sure there is. Anyway, he came and got us. Will forced Isabella to dismantle that spell on the house, and then Beren healed you. You were so burnt that no one wanted to move you. Beren insisted he heal you first."

"What about Angelica? Is she okay?"

Mum shook her head and growled. "That evil cowpat almost killed her with all those sedatives, but she'll be okay. She's in bed, resting."

"Why are we still here?"

"Will thought you might want to have better memories to take home, and we're still supposed to be vacationing, so we agreed it shouldn't stop us from trying to enjoy the rest of our holiday... that is, if you're still up to it."

I wasn't sure if I was, but I smiled anyway because I didn't want to disappoint Mum. "I sure am. I wanted to go on a gondola, and we haven't been to the Rialto Bridge yet either." Maybe if I tried hard enough, I'd convince myself?

Mum chuckled. "You always were good at bouncing back."

The door opened, and Will walked in. He halted halfway into the room, his hand still on the door, and a grin spread across his face when he saw me. He quickly shut the door and sat next to me on the other side of the bed. He kissed my forehead, lingering there for a moment before sitting up again. "How are you feeling?"

"I'm fine. Just the usual tiredness."

"Can you lie on your side so I can take a look at the back of your neck?"

That was one of the spots the snake had been touching. I did as asked. He knelt on the bed, his knees resting against my back. His fingers brushed my hair away. After a moment, he moved back and pulled my arm gently as an okay to lie on my back again. "There's only a bit of pink where it's healed. There's not going to be any scarring. Beren's a miracle worker."

"You'll get no argument from me." We were lucky to have him.

There was a knock on the door. "Come in," said Will.

Imani walked in, followed by Sarah and Lavender. "She's awake!" Imani grinned and stood at the foot of the bed, shuffling over so everyone could fit into the room.

"I am, and I'm fine. No pain."

Sarah pushed Will out of the way and leaned on the bed to give me a hug before standing next to the bed. "You had us so worried."

"I know. Sorry. And it wasn't even my fault this time."

Lavender snorted. He knew me so well.

"When Will and I got back from our evidence-gathering expedition, Isabella invited me for a drink and food. Francesco ended up joining us, and I think he almost spilled their secrets. She smashed me in the head and sent me to that house. When I came to, I went looking for Angelica, but then Isabella came back, and there was a spell on the house, so I couldn't use magic. It was a disaster."

"Well, love, we're just lucky that Francesco is a good person, or this would have had a terrible ending. He told the PIB that he didn't want to betray his grandmother—they were very close. But when he was about to step through his doorway, he realised he couldn't live with himself if she killed you. It was a struggle for him, but he made the right decision in the end."

"Thank God. He must've been so torn. Confess and have your grandmother, who practically brought you up, thrown in jail, or let her kill someone you don't know. It would have been difficult." It took some strength to stand up to her, considering he knew she was capable of murder not to mention, he loved her.

"Oh, and thanks for the clue you sent." Will raised one brow.

My forehead tightened. What was he— "Oh, that's right. I had concussion, and I vomited. I wanted you to know I was still alive, plus I needed to send it somewhere. It was stinking out the room. I thought here was as good a place as any." I grinned and sat up. Talking to everyone whilst lying down was just weird. "So, did Elena get cleared?"

"Yes," said Will. "Agent Tondato arrested Isabella. Lorenzo is also off the hook."

"So us getting those awkward photos was a waste of time."

"Yep. But it was worth it to see you blush."

"Oh, *those* photos." Lavender laughed. "You're such a perv, Lily."

My mouth dropped open. "I am not! I didn't ask for that to show up. Sheesh."

My mother grinned. "He's just having a lend."

Lavender scrunched his forehead. "A what?"

Mum chuckled. "Ah, that's right. You lot don't have that saying here. It means you were joking."

He smiled, then smirked. "Ah, right. So, were you having a lend last night when you said you didn't remember your daughter being into porn?"

My mother blushed. "I did no—" She must've realised he was kidding.

I grinned. "Don't worry, Mum. He's just having a lend." Everyone laughed. God, it was good to be enjoying a joke with this lot, even if I was the butt of it. I yawned.

Imani smiled at me. "Oh, looks like Lily needs her beauty sleep."

Mum gave me a kiss on the forehead and stood. "We'll leave you to it. We've got the gondolas booked for tomorrow morning. That gives you plenty of time to rest. Oh, and the hotel is refunding our money. Mrs Dal Lago is taking time off to deal with everything, what with her mother in jail for murder and kidnapping, and her son in jail for accessory to murder and kidnapping. They've put in another manager to run the place in the meantime. They've confirmed we can stay for the rest of our holiday."

Isabella deserved to spend the few years she had left in jail —that I could be happy about. Francesco, on the other hand, was caught up in a nightmare. Maybe he didn't even know the truth until just before we all had that last drink together? I shook my head. It wasn't my job to worry about that. The Italian PIB would get to the bottom of it, and due process would take care of the rest.

I shut my eyes for a moment to think. Did I want to go home and lick my mental wounds or not let the bad things get the better of me and stay? I blew out a breath and opened my eyes. "I guess we should stay for the rest of our break. But maybe we can take it a day at a time?"

Will took my hand and held it. "That sounds like a plan. If it's too much and you want to go home at any time, that's what we'll do."

I squeezed his hand in thanks. "What about that old woman who was turned to glass. What was the story behind that?"

Imani answered. "She was a friend of Isabella's. We found a brooch in Isabella's pocket. It was a power-enhancing device. We think she needed it to turn Mr Dal Lago, and you, into glass, but her friend was always seen wearing it, according to neighbours and local shopkeepers. We think she didn't want to hand it over when Isabella asked. So she used it to kill her and turn her into a statue—the ultimate 'up yours,' wouldn't you say?"

I sagged into the bed. "That's so sad. Bloody crazy woman."

Will nodded. "That about sums it up."

Someone knocked on the door. Lavender, who was closest, opened it. Agent Tondato came in and made it just far enough into the crowded room so the door would shut. "Good afternoon. I hope you don't mind. I wanted to see how Miss Bianchi was doing and thank you all for helping solve this case."

Well, this was a surprise. Maybe my earlier assessment of him had been as wrong as my initial assessment of Isabella. I smiled. "I'm going to be okay, thank you. I'm just really tired. And my help was accidental, if I'm honest. Everyone else's, well, they can take more credit."

Imani shook her head. "We were all scrambling like headless chickens on this one, I'm afraid."

Tondato smiled. "It is good that things turned out well. I'm sorry we could not help as much as we wanted to. We have a very difficult case at the moment that is making headlines around Italy. The people do not realise we are dealing with witches, and there have been many murders by this organisation." He frowned. "We have had much pressure from those above."

Will shook his head. "It's okay. We understand. There is never enough manpower to do everything."

"No, there is not. Ah, I also wanted to confirm that the third magic signature on Mr Dal Lago's body was Isabella's.

Our case is watertight. Francesco is going to testify against his grandmother, and with the brooch, and Lily's testimony, we have everything we need."

I swallowed. "Does that mean I have to come back for the trial?"

"Yes, but it won't be for a while. Things move slowly in Italia." He gave us a lopsided grin and shrugged. "Again, thank you for everything, and I hope you have some good holiday before you go home."

Everyone said goodbye, and he left. I yawned again. All this conversation was wearing me out. I slid down so my head was back on the pillow. Maybe I'd just shut my eyes for a little while and listen.

Lavender chuckled. "It looks like Lily is ready for another nap."

Sarah gave me a hug. "We'll see you at dinner tonight, maybe?"

I reluctantly opened my eyes. "Sounds good. Maybe a late dinner to give me time to sleep a good chunk?"

"That's a good idea," Mum said.

"Righto, peeps, Sarah and I are hitting the boutiques if anyone's interested." Lavender opened the door ready for everyone to file out. Mum gave me a huge hug and kissed my forehead, and Imani waved from the doorway. I was sad to see them all go, but man, was I exhausted. There was also a niggle in my mind that maybe I wasn't that great at dealing with the stress of murder and criminals attacking me every five minutes anymore. If it wasn't for Francesco coming back to save me, that would've been it. This time, I hadn't saved myself, and it was the closest I'd come to dying... well, maybe except for the vampire guy, but I'd beaten him in the end, which had made me feel almost invincible. My lack of caution had been a huge mistake this time. The universe had shown me that I wasn't equipped to deal with every situation. A spike of adrenaline speared through me, and a lump formed in my throat. I swallowed, but it didn't disappear.

Just breathe, Lily. Mum had been getting counselling—maybe I needed it too?

After everyone was gone, Will lay next to me and threw his arm over me, calming me somewhat. "Now go to sleep. We have dinner tonight, and then a big day planned tomorrow—even Angelica is coming. Oh, Liv and B say hello, and Angelica said to say thank you. She's probably asleep again. Liv is staying with her to make sure she's okay, and Beren is sleeping after all that healing he had to do."

I gave him a tired smile. Focussing on my loved ones was just the therapy I could use right now. "Oh, good. I'm glad she really is okay. It was horrific seeing her unresponsive." I turned on my side to face Will. "Why can't life just be easy?"

"I don't know, Lily. But right now, we're all safe, so let's concentrate on that. We just have to enjoy every good moment when it comes." He leaned closer, his lips meeting mine, his citrussy shampoo scent filling my nose. This must be one of those moments he meant. Hmm, it wouldn't be hard to take his wise advice.

Not hard at all.

SIGN UP TO MY NEWSLETTER

Thank you so much for reading Westerham Witches and a Venetian Vendetta. If you enjoyed it and plan on reading more of my books, you might want to sign up to my newsletter. You'll receive news of my upcoming books, new releases, and sales, and every now and then you'll receive free bonus material, such as short stories or unpublished scenes. I promise not to spam you, and you can always easily unsubscribe. If you'd like to sign up, just click HERE, which will take you to my website and the signup page.

I hope to see you there soon!

Also, just a little note to tell you that there will be a PIB book 16 coming in May 2021. I just don't know what it's called yet :). Cheers!

ALSO BY DIONNE LISTER

Paranormal Investigation Bureau

The Circle of Talia

(YA Epic Fantasy)

Realm of Blood and Fire

The Rose of Nerine

(Epic Fantasy)

Tempering the Rose

ABOUT THE AUTHOR

USA Today bestselling author, Dionne Lister is a Sydneysider with a degree in creative writing, two Siamese cats, and is a member of the Science Fiction and Fantasy Writers of America. Daydreaming has always been her passion, so writing was a natural progression from staring out the window in primary school, and being an author was a dream she held since childhood.

Unfortunately, writing was only a hobby while Dionne worked as a property valuer in Sydney, until her mid-thirties when she returned to study and completed her creative writing degree. Since then, she has indulged her passion for writing while raising two children with her husband. Her books have attracted praise from Apple iBooks and have reached #1 on Amazon and iBooks charts worldwide, frequently occupying top 100 lists in fantasy. She's excited to add cozy mystery to the list of genres she writes. Magic and danger are always a heady combination.

Printed in Great Britain
by Amazon

75908705R00118